Praise for *A Heart Full Of Hope*

"I was shocked when I received the call that there were Twins on the ground. It has been fun to watch them grow. They are truly a miracle!"
~Christina Dayton, DVM

"The story of the BoGo twins simply captured my heart. For readers such as me who were completely ignorant of horses as I began the fascinating journey of the foals, Jennifer succinctly, yet effectively, ensured that I could not only comprehend but appreciate the miraculous story of the twins. This beautifully written novel will surely become one of your favorites!"
~Amanda Hurd

"I was captivated from the first posting by the drama of twin Arabian foals playing out in my Facebook newsfeed. Their story is both magical and mesmerizing!! I hope to watch them grow up together!"
~Ramona Trusty

Jennifer Wilson

First published in 2016

First paperback edition by Bookbaby™, 2016

Library of Congress Cataloging in Publication Number:

Print ISBN: 978-1-48356-761-7
eBook ISBN: 978-1-48356-762-4

Printed in the United States of America by Bookbaby™

A Heart Full of Hope

Hope

The Tale of the Twin Arabian Colts

Jennifer Wilson

Jennifer Wilson

To My Readers:

Words cannot express how grateful I am that you have picked up this memoir and are about to experience my early journey with Majus and Majician, also known as The BOGO Colts. BOGO, in case you are not much of a shopper, is an acronym for Buy One, Get One (as in Free). This fond nickname was dubbed them by my mother the day they were born and, although their journey is much more than "getting one free", it has stuck. If you are not familiar with horses, you may be wondering why a tale about twin Arabian colts is so fascinating and memoir-worthy.

The simple truth is that horses are not designed to carry, deliver, and nourish twins. Although as many as 1 in 10 equine pregnancies may result in the conception of twins, most are absorbed or aborted before six weeks. When a mare carries twins beyond a month, a staggering 80% of those pregnancies end in abortion, even into the eighth month. Well over half of the remaining twin pregnancies will still result in late term abortion or still birth. You should understand that even when a mare gives birth to a live, viable set of twins, less than 20% of those will actually survive to their second week of life. To put it simply, a set of surviving twins is about a one in a million chance.

Now, those of you who are familiar with horse breeding may be thinking, *What an irresponsible breeder to not have that poor mare sonogrammed!* Worry not, dear reader! This mare was sonogrammed before breeding, confirming a single follicle. She was again sonogrammed after breeding (a single live cover) confirming a single ovulation. At two weeks, she was confirmed in foal with a *single* embryo. How did this happen? We actually don't know. They were on the same side of the uterus in a single placenta- all the signs pointing to identical. However, DNA results confirm they are not identical. Their extremely similar size at birth combined with the fact they were born two weeks early denounce the possibility of a subsequent ovulation a week or so later that met up with some very vital and very long-lived sperm. In many senses of the way, they are miracles.

With the technicalities aside, I now want you to understand one thing very clearly. While this book is written like a dreamy, happy ever after novel, it is a true story. I changed the names only of my immediate family because I want the focus on the journey, not the persons. Most of the other people involved with them were happy to see their real names as they were integral parts of this amazing adventure. Spoiler alert, you may want to skip to the next paragraph. My third mare was really confirmed in foal on my birthday. I really found out my family was expecting our own third child on January third. We really sold our house after six days on the market and moved into a new home with three pregnant mares about to burst. Mark really was completing stalls as mares were having babies. The twins really arrived on my wedding anniversary. They truly almost died from a blood infection and were saved by the amazing staff at New Bolton Center. The horrifying drive at midnight while my husband was out of town, in the old farm truck, in the rain, to get them to New Bolton really happened. A lot of people we didn't even know sent us incredible donations to assist because they believed in the colts and in my dreams. Sweetie really had her colt outside just two days after the epic New Bolton journey. I really sold their dam, Mona, to keep the farm afloat. I really sold at least one (at the time of printing, the second is on the market) of my incredible half Arabian foals to keep the dream alive. I really wrote this book not only to give back to those who believed, but to share the possibility of dreams and the beauty of life. I also really wrote this book to make the improbable dream of a lifetime with these colts a reality. And, I was really, truly, honestly pregnant in my mid-thirties with my third until these colts were three months old.

Because this is a completely true story with only some of the dialogue fabricated (my memory isn't *that* good) the plot structure doesn't quite follow the traditional literary organization. I was limited in the use of symbolism and I couldn't get too tricky with the theme. Because it was real life events, they were simply what they were. The heavy action happens pretty early in the story and I chose to bring this particular book to a speedy closing. I could have gone into far greater detail about our family life- fitting in Pop Warner football and Cub Scouts, trying to get our stinky goat on the trailer to sell him (that was an adventure all its own), an a million and one other little details and activities that fill a story up. But I didn't. For one, it was real life and after the boys survived and all of the foals arrived, not much more happened than just life. I was pretty miserable towards the end of my pregnancy and I didn't want to drone on and on about my swollen ankles and aching back. Nor did I want to make anything up for the sake of a story. I kept this true to life. Furthermore, I was on a crazy self-set deadline. My husband was running out of patience and I needed to make something magical happen. Fast. And while holding down a demanding job and trying to be as good a mother as possible with three young children. I hope I have the opportunity in the future to write a real fiction because this was an incredible experience an left me wanting to have the freedom to write complete fiction. The images in this story are less than perfect; they are actual, impromptu cell phone photos for the most part, never intended for print in a real novel. Enjoy them for the moments in time that they captured. This story has a main conflict (the colts' survival) and a secondary conflict (our ability to keep them or at least ensure they remained together.)

Although the secondary conflict is complicated by finances, I don't want people to think that we are not in a position to care for our horses. The simple truth is we are in a time of growth (which is a good thing) and I had a plan. Well, to be honest, I had two plans. I had the plan I told my husband and my little internal accountant and I had the "secret plan" that was locked away in my very hopeful heart. The main plan from the beginning of 2015 was to phase out our purebred program and focus on our wildly successful Half Arabian program. We would be honored with a filly from Mona, my last purebred mare. I would sell this filly overseas for a good chunk of change seeing as the stallion had already sired a yearling filly who was lighting up the international arenas and the mare had already had a filly that had been exported to Jordan. I also told my husband hopefully Mona would sell in a package or in a separate sale for a decent amount. With these funds, I would retain my Half Arabian foals and help pay off the next five acres in our farm expansion. The secret heart plan was that the filly would sell for so much that I would just put Mona out on a breeding lease for a season or two while we were expanding and then I bring her back home. Hey, it was a business plan, complete with a plan B. Probably not very realistic, but I have always been a dreamer. I have always had a heart full of hope and faith that things will work. I have also been blessed because for the most part, things have always eventually worked out for the best, or even better than the best. When I found out I was expecting our third child, we moved from our modest doublewide into a far roomier split level, complete with garage, basement, and attic. I am in storage heaven. We also expanded from five acres to fifteen acres with an additional five we still need to purchase and our wandering eye on the adjoining ten acres. Growth is good, but it is tough and it is not conducive to a breeding program that consistently takes a loss regardless of extremely high success rates of the progeny. There were many, many hopes sitting on Mona's filly. And then I walked out the first morning of summer break to discover twin colts. Both Plan A and Plan B were dashed out the window. I have had several ideas since and countless supporters. This book is somewhere around Plan XYZ, I think.

Although I am a high school English teacher who is a voracious reader and blessed with a bit of a knack for the written word, this was a difficult novel for me to write. It wasn't hard in the aspect of getting the memories into words; actually, the words of this book have flowed out of my fingertips into the print you are currently reading as if they were living beings with a destiny and a purpose. Rather, reliving these experiences has been hard. Many of these chapters were written with sentences swimming on the screen. In several of the read-aloud edits hosted by my very patient mother, I choked up and the words failed to exit my throat. During my own revising and editing, on more than one occasion, I sat with tears fully streaming down my face. It was so hard. I am blessed to be chosen to experience this journey, and I am blessed to share it with you. So, go grab a box of Kleenex, and enjoy.

Thank you

A story such as this cannot proceed without a multitude of personal thank yous. I have worked on this list for weeks, and yet I fear someone may be missed. If I have missed you in print, please accept my apologies and know that I have never missed you in my heart.

Thank you to each and every fan who has followed Majus and Majician on Facebook- all 11,000 of you at the time of the first printing.

Thank you to those of you who helped fund their initial vet fees and those who began and participated in the "keep the colts" drive. You have inspired me beyond imagine, and because of you, this book exists.

Thank you to my amazing colleagues this year who dealt with my maternity, my many distractions and listened for hours on end as I yammered out my hopes and dreams.

Thank you to Mr. Clarke who has always made me chin up, look in the mirror, and see my own self-worth.

Thank you to the Wolfes for all of the foals you have halter broken, the years of support, and for helping me begin the dream of the "Big Time".

Thank you to Joe Alberti, Rob Janecki, Maddy Winer, Amelia Hruban, and all of the Maghnus Z+// family who made me realize my breeding program has value. Your belief and support has helped keep me going through the tough years.

Thank you to David Conner and Miller Pinson. You have supported me beyond all belief over the three months of the writing of this book. You have taken my horses and my family as a part of your own. You have encouraged. You have cheered. You have rooted and gone far above and beyond. We will go farther!

Thank you to all of the veterinarians who helped keep these boys alive. Your tremendous efforts, advice, and care made this dream live on.

Thank you, Kerry! You have always been here, even from a great distance. For everything.

Thank you Jamie, we never grew out of the little girl dreams!

Thank you to my very non- horsey best friend, Nicole, for understanding why I tend to fall off the edge of the earth for a couple of months at a time while I am occupied with chasing rainbows. You know I always come back.

Thank you to Stephanie and Sonya. For the hours of mutual dreaming. For the horses, the dirt, the ribbons, and the pictures. For the sweat and tears. For the laughter and the sobs. For the past and the future.

Thank you to Jim, my stepfather, who made nothing more than a dream become a reality. Thank you for the training, the advice, the dreaming and the belief.

Thank you to my Mom. No matter how good it was, you always pushed me to go farther. Your love and support took me through the roughest and darkest times of my life and through the brightest times. Thank you for the US and Canadian Nationals trips, including all of the adventures (and misadventures!). Thank you for the belief that you always have in me. Thank you for sharing the broken hearts and the national champion dreaming. Thank you for listening to the verbal edits of this book twenty times over. Thank you for being my mom.

Thank you to my babies, Austin, Kate, and Savannah. I hope someday you understand how amazing you are to me. It probably won't be until you have babies of your own.

Thank you to Mark. You have been more of a husband than any woman could dream of. You have tirelessly loved me. You have supported me through career changes, late-life bachelors and masters degrees. You have handled my whimsical heart like no one else. You are the best father ever. You may not understand my dreamer personality, but you believe in me regardless. I am secure in your love.

Thank you God. Thank you for the trials you have given me throughout my life that shaped who I am. Thank you for the ceaseless blessings with which you have bestowed upon me. Thank you for the talents you have honored me with so that I can share the incredible stories you have created for my life.

Jennifer Wilson

"Go confidently in
the direction of your
dreams. Live the life
you've imagined."

~ Henry David Thoreau

Jennifer Wilson

This book is dedicated to those who have believed and to all who dare to dream.

Prologue

August 17th

"Congratulations! You have a baby! This makes three foals next year, right?" Dr. Dayton smiled cheerfully as she wiped down and sanitized her sonogram wand and cord.

"Yes," Jessica Williams beamed with pride. *Three! Three healthy pregnancies! What a busy summer we will have. It is a good thing we decided to hold out on moving for one more year. I will sell the purebred foal and hopefully keep both Half Arabian babies.* She pushed her long, dark brown bangs out of her face and took a deep breath as her heart pounded in her chest. "I am so excited about this. It will certainly be a challenge training three foals but I am going to have a blast next summer now that Aiden and Kat will finally be old enough that I can really spend more time with my horses again!"

The two-and-a-half-year-old Kat, supervised by the family Australian Shepherd, Bandit, was happily digging in the dirt out in the round pen. Aiden, who had just turned seven, was observing intently outside the stall door. His heart smiled to learn that all three mares were going to have foals next summer. This time around, finally, they would keep one, maybe two of them.

Jess gazed dreamily across the pasture at the chestnut Purebred Arabian mare, PA A-Magic Moment and the exquisite coal-black Half Arabian mare, Penelope Rose RF, both already confirmed in foal. She then kissed the soft muzzle of her senior broodmare, The Sweet Rose, who was a sister to the young Penelope. Sweetie's progeny had thus far all been champions at the Regional show level or higher. Her foals have thus far included the unstoppable Maghnus Z, the most successful Half-Arabian halter horse in history by age seven and by age eight had won an unprecedented seventeen champion or reserve champion titles at the National Arabian horse shows. The foal she was carrying would be a three-quarter sibling and destined for greatness; the sire was just exported to Palestine, and this would be his only Half Arabian foal. Furthermore, Sweetie would be nineteen years old when this foal arrived. There would be very few, if any, more opportunities to retain a foal from her. *Happy Birthday to me...* Jess mused happily. She had waited nearly a decade to be in a position to keep a foal that she bred, and she just knew this one would be beyond special.

January 3rd

Trembling hands held the slim white stick as a plus sign developed in the tiny window.

Plus... plus. Plus means positive. Positive. Oh my Lord. I'm pregnant. We're having number three. How... What... THREE children! How exciting! ...I cannot believe I just found that old "Congratulations" glitter while vacuuming this morning! Isn't that just serendipitous... You will get a kick out of this, Nicole! My Lord, I'm too old; how will I do this in my mid-thirties? I'm pregnant...we need a bigger house. Now! In no way can we fit a family of five in this tiny box... We need to sell this place and move. Oh my Lord, I have three pregnant mares. I said I would never do this again- pregnant with pregnant mares... I can't do this with three new foals this summer...

Chapter One

June 17th

The chestnut mare lazily swished her copper tail in the early-summer heat and shifted her weight on her swollen rear ankles. Although this was her fourth pregnancy and she was fairly young, she was more uncomfortable than she had ever before been. Something was different this time; just this morning, she nearly fell while walking from her stall, her ligaments were so loose. A fly buzzed monotonously near and attempted to rest on her velvet nose. She wearily flapped her lower lip and the nuisance droned away. With a deep sigh, she shifted her weight again. Her huge, dark eyes closed to the glare of the afternoon sun and she rested.

Three days ago, she went off of her feed. She simply wasn't hungry and, besides, she felt there was no room in her abdomen for even the smallest bite. Her person, The Woman, also heavily pregnant, watched with concern as the mare apathetically nosed her meals over the past several days. She had known the mare to fast prior to foaling, but never this early; she had still had over three weeks to go when she began acting strangely.

They had moved from their old home a short five weeks prior. Although the new home was much larger and had substantially more land for pasture, it was still without a barn for the horses. The Man, a carpenter by trade, was building as fast as he could while working and helping his family unpack and move furniture. Just under three weeks ago, he completed framing out the three stall shed-style barn and finished the foaling stall in the nick of time. The black mare had foaled that night. The chestnut mare drank in another deep breath and noted with satisfaction that The Man had completed building the third stall this afternoon. Last week, The Woman had moved the young black mare and her filly out of the larger foaling stall so the chestnut mare could move in. That was good, for she did not feel that her body would hold out much longer; she could hardly believe that just a few weeks ago she was trying to steal a peanut butter and jelly sandwich from The Boy and The Girl. She sighed and her flank quivered almost in response.

For two weeks, although she was a teacher who woke before the crack of dawn, had two children, and was expecting a third, The Woman had set her alarm each night at 11:00 pm and again at 2:00 am to check on the chestnut mare. The farm was located behind a dark, winding trail through dense woods that stood solidly between the home and the horse property. The path was bumpy and the ground twisted and treacherous with exposed roots from decades of traffic made by The Man's family for the previous four decades. It was early for the mare, too early, but The

Woman didn't like the way she was acting; thus, The Woman lumbered through the difficult path night after night, nervously rubbing her swollen belly with every trip as the narrow beam from the flashlight bounced with each step. However, this day was the last professional day of school for the exhausted teacher. By evening, The Pregnant Woman was so spent she failed to set her alarm. She slept.

Around midnight, when the great horned owls were hooting mysteriously in the trees, the pains came. The chestnut mare pawed in her fresh straw, turned in circles, laid down, and got back up. So it began. Yet, she felt something was different this time. As the pains intensified, she readied herself to become a mother again. And a glorious mother she was with exquisite offspring, including a filly that had been exported overseas. With a deep groan, she sank to her knees and then rolled onto her side. She knew the labor was difficult and she began her work. To her surprise, the foal began slipping out with hardly a push. How could it be so easy? Before the mare had time to register, she was gripped with another contraction and she felt more. What was this? She leaned up with strands of golden straw glistening in her long mane and turned her elegant neck to see what she had created.

Chapter Two

June 15th

"One. Two. One. Two. Oh my Lord, Mona, what have you done?" Jessica, who always had her mares sonogrammed to detect a twin pregnancy early, raised one shaking hand to her gaping mouth while the other absently began rubbing her swollen belly. Large tears welled in her disbelieving eyes. She was staring at two tiny chestnut bodies nestled next to each other deep in the straw. Mona, standing comfortably in the strewn bedding, looked at Jessica with deep satisfaction and nuzzled the nearest miracle. Within moments, both twins were up on their spindly legs and nursing.

After the initial shock passed, Jess noted that they were dry, and by the sound of the eager guzzling and slurping, they had already become expert nursers. This miraculous event had happened several hours earlier. They were oh-so-tiny. Each one looked to weigh no more than 50 or 60 pounds. Jess mused that the gentlest breeze of summer would knock them right off their feet. *How could they possibly be alive and nursing,* she wondered in amazement. *They ARE alive! They are ALIVE!* Her brain shouted at her, bringing her out of her trance.

Trembling hands almost dropped her slim cell phone and she had to tap her husband's number three times before she got it right. "Matt? Matt! Get out here, there are two!" she breathed into the phone. She felt as if the air had been slammed out of her lungs.

Jessica was a tiny woman of thirty six. Her thirty-seventh birthday loomed around the corner. As her grandmother on her father's side, she preferred to wear her dark brown hair as long as possible. Because of the horses, it was often corralled into a ponytail. Her diminutive size and tendency to wear a ponytail made her appear younger than her years. Jess had lived an enchanted life. As a young girl not old enough for school, she rode a pony at a fair and was instantly infected with a passion for the equine. Without fail, she penned ***Pony*** at the top of every wish list. Unfortunately, it was a wish her single mother, previous pony owner and also born with the apparently genetic equine addiction syndrome, could not fulfill at the time. Upon her eighth year, Jess's mother met a man. This man happened to have a small Arabian horse farm. Before long, that man was Jess's stepfather and she was literally living her dreams. Although very smart in school, Jess felt she didn't need college and she certainly wasn't going to pay for the whole thing. She was bitter that her participation in equine activities and shows did not equate to extracurricular activities on scholarship applications and she was dismayed to watch her school-affiliated-sports-peers raking in all of the financial aid. She spent the next several years waitressing and bartending at her local beach town, Rehoboth, and became a foodie. In that time, she dated a musician and had brief run ins with several amazing musical artists and even tapped glasses with some soon-to-be-on-the-radio bands. She wouldn't have changed those days for a million dollars; however, her heart longed for what she had left behind. So she came back home, all of twenty-five minutes into rural Delaware. There she found an honest, hands-on, family man husband. A mere ninety days before their wedding, she called him at work to tell him he had three weeks to build a run in and pasture on their prim little five acres because she had bought a horse. Jessica sold her first car, a 1981 Camaro (on which she had gone through three engines before a 400 small block handled her exuberance behind the wheel) to purchase the grey mare. Matt Williams, in love with that crazy girl, obliged. In April, she brought home The Sweet Rose. By the time she had her son in 2007 Jess knew she needed a career. A real job. Bartending just wouldn't cut it anymore. At the ripe age of thirty, she sucked it up, applied for student loans, and began her teaching degree at Wilmington University. Determined to get school out of the way, Jess pounded through her undergraduate and then graduate courses, earning both a Bachelor's and a Master's Degree in just over four years. During the last semester of her undergraduate degree, she gave birth to their second child, a daughter. After teaching a year in the third grade, she eventually secured a job at the local high school from which her husband graduated. She had a great husband, a boy, a girl, a third child on the way, a dog, a few Arabian horses, a promising future, and life was perfect.

"Two what? Jess, what are you talking about?" Matt asked in confusion.

"There are two foals here. Oh my God, there are two. And they're alive! Get out here!"

"What? I don't... Oh Lord, yes, yes, honey, I'm on my way", Matt exclaimed as the reality of the miraculous situation dawned on his pre-coffee mind.

Five minutes later, there they stood, holding hands, and they watched for a magical moment the miracles that were breathing and taking nourishment from their dam right before their eyes. "Happy anniversary, baby," Jessica sighed. Matt, a full foot taller, gently squeezed her delicate hand.

Matt was a year younger than Jess. He was the classic country son of a prison guard and a registered nurse. He came from a hard working and God-fearing family and he held tight to classic American family ideals in a generation of growing recklessness. Like Jess, he was quiet in his youth. Matt was brilliant in the mathematics department. Like Rainman smart. As did Jess, he favored fast cars. He wrapped his Monte Carlo around a tree when he was only sixteen. The investigating officers said it was by the grace of his Guardian Angel that he walked away. They never believed him when he swore he was not wearing his seatbelt. He grew up in a small town and, like his oldest sister, went away to the big college at High Point in North Carolina. He graduated with a degree in computer information systems at the peak of the technological boom and took a dream internship with Dell in Boston. Six months later, lines from Office Space were echoing in his head; he was losing his mind in that tiny little cubicle and he returned home to work for his uncle as a general contractor. The hard labor made his young body strong and his skin tan. When Jess saw the six-foot-one-inch young man walk her way, her heart was gone for the rest of her life. By the time he married her, Matt realized Jess was a dreamer but his heart was also already long gone. She was like him in that there wasn't a lazy bone in her body, and he knew she always tried hard to self-support her dreams. However, she never was able to do so without his assistance. So, for years, he patiently supported her. He never imagined her dreams would live to encompass twin colts.

After a few moments of savoring the moment, Jessica sprang to action and once again frantically tapped the screen on her cell phone.

"Hello, Dr. Dayton? This is Jess Williams. Mona foaled last night. She had twins… Yes, they are both alive. Yes they are nursing right now...Really? … Yes, I dug out the placenta, but it is pretty trampled and torn up… it's in a bucket waiting for your exam… Yes, I'll be here all day…. Ok, thank you, see you this afternoon." Jess immediately called her mother then her best horse friend and supporter, Stephanie, while Matt called his father. Naturally, she next texted those closest to her and finally hit social media with the announcement of the miracles. She posted some quick cell phone shots and requested prayers for continued health. In cyberspace, a whirlwind fury of interest began to grow over the rare little pair, as of yet still unnamed.

*　　*　　*

Inside the split-level house that Matt grew up in, Aiden woke and leisurely stretched his almost-eight-year-old frame. Aiden was a curious boy. He was very intelligent, but equally sensitive. Like both of his parents, he was intelligent, but shy around his peers. For his entire life, he had seemed to understand far more than was natural for his years. He was frequently quiet and brooding. He questioned the honesty of the human race and did not understand how people could so often be so cruel to each other. Aiden was generally shorter than his like-aged peers, a trait he inherited from his tiny mother. However, what he lacked in height, he made up for in handsome boy looks. Large, wide-set eyes peered out from ridiculously thick, long lashes. His sandy hair was soft and short while a smattering of freckles frolicked over his high cheek bones. Already, he was developing strong, square shoulders and a deep chest.

With a satisfying stretch, Aiden crawled out of bed and wandered to the bathroom, scratching his morning hair. Morning routine completed, he made his way downstairs and realized it was unusually quiet in the house. *Where is everyone*, he wondered. He wandered back upstairs to confirm that his three year old sister, Kat, was still blissfully in dreamland. Her golden curls encircled her head like a cherub's halo around her pillow and she sighed contentedly in her slumber, subconsciously aware that someone was in her room. From downstairs, he heard the bang of the front door and excited voices. He gently closed her door and then raced down the stairs to determine the meaning of all of the commotion.

"Mom, what's going on," he asked, golden brown eyes glowing and feeding off of his parents' buzz. He felt giddy although he had no idea what was going on.

"Mona had her babies last night," Jess responded, grabbing his fair hair and kissing the top of his head.

"Babies?" he asked in confusion, knowing horses are not designed to have twins and that his parents always had a sonogram on the mares to ensure only one foal early in the pregnancy. Once, he had innocently asked what happened when there were two, but he did not understand when his mother explained that the vet would "pinch one off". It sounded terrible, and he preferred not to ponder the specifics of that particular inquiry.

"Yes honey, twins".

Aiden's little heart sank. *Surely they are not alive, that never happens or they would not have to check for it,* he thought. He supposed they were excited because maybe Mona survived the birthing of the twins.

Immediately seeing the concern on her gentle boy's crumpled little face, Jessica reached out a soft hand and ruffled his summer-sandy-brown hair. "They're fine, honey. They're all alive and well!"

Aiden immediately cheered and shouted as he tore up the stairs, "I'm getting dressed!! I'm going out to see them!!" Aside from his puppy and pony, and maybe his little sister, he couldn't recall a more exciting moment in his yet-brief life.

*   *   *

After a few hours, Dr. Dayton arrived to perform the post-foaling exam. She was amazed by the golden cherubs napping in the straw.

"Oh my gosh," she whispered. "Look at those markings… They look identical!" Dr. Dayton marveled over their similarity in size and in their nearly identical blazes and stockings. With wonderment and the grin of a young girl at her first carnival, the gentle vet and her assistant quietly entered the stall. She stepped softly over to the colts, who were still nestled in the clean bedding and began her examination.

After determining that their lungs and heart sounded healthy, she checked general vitals by their eyes and gums. Satisfied that they were quite healthy, she then drew blood from each colt to run the IGG test which measured the strength of the antibodies they received from their mother's milk. The test results hit the magical 800 mark, which generally ensured the foals' immune systems would be strong enough to survive the outside world.

Done with the twins' checkups, Dr. Dayton then turned her attentions to the mare. "Has she been normal? Drinking? Passing stool, showing any signs of discomfort?"

"She seems happy," Jess reported. "She's been drinking her water and I have not seen unusual discharge. But, there has been no manure since she had the babies."

"That is probably not abnormal considering what she just went through. It must have been quite traumatic on her system," Dr. Dayton caressed the mare's sleek neck and performed a visual check on her. "I think we should oil her just to be on the safe

Jennifer Wilson

side," she said after listening to Mona's digestive through her stethoscope.

Jess agreed, and in a few minutes, a long, soft tube was threaded into Mona's stomach from her nostril. The vet pumped in some warm water mixed with mineral oil and then gently pulled the tube back out.

"She will be much more comfortable soon. If you don't see any manure by tonight, give me a call. Now, you said you have the placenta in a bucket?"

"Yes," Jess answered, stepping into the little tack room. She returned with an old, cracked bucket no longer suitable for holding water. The flies seemed to have taken a special interest in this bucket and buzzed angrily at the disturbance.

Dr. Dayton pulled on fresh gloves, dumped the contents of the bucket on the ground in front of the small barn and began to stretch out the thick membrane that had provided life for the twins during the eleven months that they developed inside their mother's womb.

A grayish-purple in color, the placenta was shaped vaguely like a Rorschach bat. Dr. Dayton noted that it was healthy in color and thickness and then pondered over it for a few minutes before speaking.

"I just don't understand this. They should have been on different sides of her uterus. Generally twins will occur from an

Jennifer Wilson

ovulation on each side and a foal settles in each the left and the right horns. But I can clearly see where each umbilicus was attached here, on this side. They don't appear to be a result of separate left/right ovulations. How many times was she covered, Jess?"

Jess, knowing that horses simply do not have identical twins replied. "She was only bred one time. She was ultrasounded the day before the breeding. She has a single follicle developing on the right side. Her left side was empty. She was also ultrasounded after the cover and it showed a single ovulation. You don't think they are identical, do you?"

"If I were you, I would get them DNA tested," Dr. Dayton murmured in awe.

*   *   *

The remainder of the morning and that afternoon were a frenzy of texts, phone calls, visitors and media updates. The boys, as of yet unnamed, were quickly becoming famous. Finally, in the late afternoon, Jessica sank her weary body into the rocking chair that had been the favorite of her mother-in-law. She rubbed her dreadfully swollen ankles and called her mother again, who had to work that morning and had not been able to come to the farm.

"Well honey," Janine said candidly to her only daughter, "Looks like you got BoGo colts."

"Bogo, Mom?" Jess asked in dazed exhaustion, sliding a dirty hand across a dusty forehead.

"Yes, dear, Buy One, Get One!"

A warm smile stretched across Jess's face and she glowed as the reality of the day hit. "Yes," she giggled, "BoGo Colts".

"How do they look… how is Mona?"

"She's amazing, doesn't even look like she had a foal- they're tiny, but incredible. They really couldn't look any healthier. And they are so freaking *pretty*! The blood work for antibodies came back great- not off the charts like Sweetie's foals, but really good. They are very curious and Mona has been a gem! Dr. Dayton said she's not even sure how Mona delivered them, she looks like nothing even happened" Jessica replied, absentmindedly rubbing her belly and feeling her own baby give a light kick in response.

"What are you planning on naming them?" Janine inquired.

"I've been thinking, Mom. You know how Mona's name is PA A-Magic Moment and the sire is Majd Alrabi? Well, I am thinking of naming the bigger one Majus, for wise man… but spelled with a "j" instead of a "g"… and the little one Majician, because it's magic that he survived. The Wise Man and the Magician. What do you think?"

Jess heard the approval in her mother's voice, "I *love* it, honey!"

Jess continued, "I received about three hundred friend requests on my Facebook account today. Crazy. Megan Warnick... Do you know my friend Megan? She was Miss Delaware last year and she also does photography? Well, she suggested I create a page just for them. She thinks they will become famous and that my personal page will become completely overwhelmed. Can you believe that?"

"I think it's a great idea, Jess," Janine concurred. The women chatted on happily as Jessica stroked her belly and smiled as she felt the baby squirming around. She could hear Kat babbling her princess stories to her Daddy downstairs.

Meanwhile, Aiden lay curled on his bed, hugging an old pillow and brooding silently. These colts were amazing. But his parents had *never* kept a single foal they bred. Each one was a champion, some were making history at the Arabian shows. Yet he couldn't understand why they always sold them; usually before they were even a year old. Surely, his parents wouldn't sell miracles, would they? Although he had his own Half Arabian pony he loved dearly, his tender heart broke a little more with every beautiful foal that was born and sold. He heaved a young boy's sorrowful sigh as a delicate tear traced its way down his sweet cheek.

Jennifer Wilson

Chapter Three

June 15th

Evening

The late afternoon sun burned into the golden straw that so deeply bedded the foaling stall. The mare dozed contentedly in the late afternoon warmth and swished quietly at the occasional fly buzzing by. She had passed her post foaling exam and her stomach was much more comfortable. Her colts' blood work came back adequate in much-needed antibodies. Two tiny bodies shimmered with health in the glow of late afternoon, and one was using the other as a pillow. There they napped contentedly, tiny tails flicking on occasion, their little bellies full of their mother's warm milk, for she was an excellent producer. That evening was a little piece of heaven, right there, in that hand-made-with-love stall. Outside, the black mare's month old filly danced in the bold sunlight and the old grey queen broodmare sighed deeply and shifted the weight on her uncomfortable ankles as the chestnut mare had done just the day before. She had two and a half more weeks until her due date. The grasshoppers whirred dreamily in the grass as a bald eagle sailed silently above.

Chapter Four

June 19th

It was Day Two, and Majus and Majician appeared to be thriving. Stephanie arrived at the farm right after breakfast; the boys had a big day ahead of them.

As Stephanie slipped the halter on Mona's lovely head, the twins gulped greedily, on occasion knocking each other away, but essentially sharing. Jessica proudly scratched the fragile bodies that were already filling in from their mother's milk. The larger one, Majus, was dreadfully weak in the pasterns, but this was something she had seen from time to time in normal foals. She vowed to keep the faith that they would, in time, strengthen. Their beautiful heads were so big on their tiny bodies, but, true to their Arabian heritage, they had the most exquisitely sculpted ears with tips that turned in so they looked like tiny horns. *Look at how their blazes are almost exactly the same, and how their front socks are matching. How delicate their muzzles are and their large eyes are set so nice and low on wide foreheads. What will they look like when they are grown? How big will the get? Will all of their parts balance out?* Jess wondered in awe.

With droplets of milk glistening on their delicate whiskers, the colts peered fearlessly at the two humans in their stall with open curiosity.

"Are you ready? Do you have your phone out?" Stephanie asked.

"Of course," Jessica excitedly replied. "Let's go!"

Stephanie swung the stall door open and slowly lead Mona out of the stall. She waited patiently while the two colts who had become adept at scampering around their tiny domain both tripped and stumbled over the edge of the doorway. Mona gave a concerned nicker and in a flash, the delicate little colts were on their feet and surveying the world around them. The summer pests were quick to find their soft flesh and their thin tails flicked back and forth. They breathed deeply the fresh air and bumbled forward. Mona nickered encouragingly.

In a tangle of legs, they were bouncing across the pasture. Eight spindly legs flew in every which direction and Mona's nickers of encouragement turned towards concern as they scampered farther away.

"Easy, girl," Stephanie reassured her, stroking her long, luxurious mane. Mona nosed her nervously as Jessica recorded the precious footage. Aiden and Kat clapped their hands in delight while the little miracles perambulated their way around their

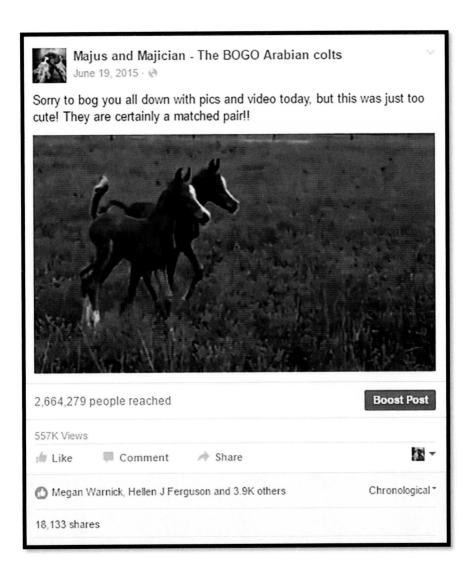

Majus and Majician - The BOGO Arabian colts
June 19, 2015 ·

Sorry to bog you all down with pics and video today, but this was just too cute! They are certainly a matched pair!!

2,664,279 people reached

Boost Post

557K Views

Like   Comment   Share

Megan Warnick, Hellen J Ferguson and 3.9K others   Chronological

18,133 shares

mother, sniffing the new found grass and snorting at the grasshoppers and gnats.

After Stephanie led Mona back to the stall and the boys were contentedly nursing again, little sides heaving from the excitement and exercise, the four humans (two standing on a lawn chair) gazed admiringly over the stall door at the beautiful scene before them.

"It's amazing," Stephanie said.

"It feels unreal," Jess replied.

"Mommy," Aiden questioned, turning his soft eyes up to his mother, "will they live?"

"I don't know, Sweetie. I just can't say. They look good now, better than good, but I won't breathe easy until they are at least two months old. You know the chances both twins in horses surviving are about one in a million."

"I really hope they make it."

"Me, too, honey. Me, too."

*   *   *

Later that evening, Matt packed his bags to head out of town for business over the weekend.

As she gazed lovingly up at the man who had worked so hard to support her horse craze, Jess implored, "Hurry home, this is

50

wearing on me. It's a bit more excitement than I feel I can handle. Plus, you need to finish the last stall; Sweetie looks like she will pop any second now."

"Sweetie always looks like she's about to pop. I'll do my best," Matt promised, both knowing he wouldn't be able to make it home until Sunday evening.

Chapter Five

June 19th

Evening

After settling the kids in with an evening movie, Jess fired up her old laptop and logged onto Facebook. She was barraged with hundreds more friend requests; all strangers interested in her little miracles. Jess took a deep breath, deleted them all, and clicked on "Create Page" under her Facebook account. She nibbled distractedly on her bottom lip for a moment before choosing the title "Majus and Majician- The BoGo Arabian Colts". She clicked on the profile square and browsed through the various cell phone shots that had been snapped over the past two days. Finally, she chose the close-up shot of them nursing from the same side that Stephanie had captured and texted to her. It was an amazing image, and had potential to become iconic of the twins' deep attachment to each other. She then looked for a wallpaper image and settled down to write the content.

Jessica began the page with a post addressing frequently asked questions she anticipated would come up. She noticed throughout the day that some of the photos that had been shared had gone semi-viral and that people could be absolutely venomous regarding situations about which they did not have all of the

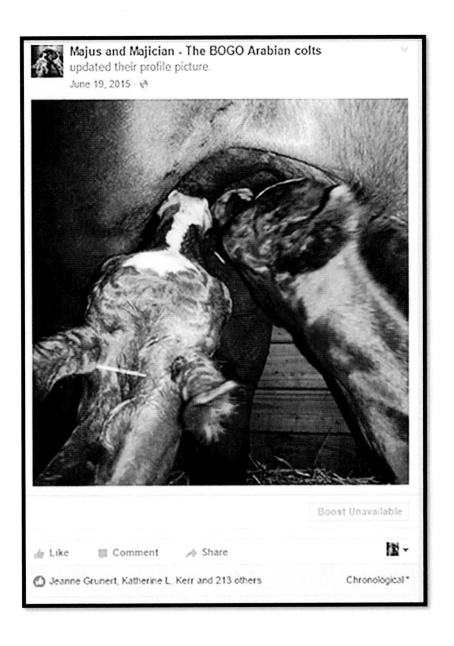

Majus and Majician - The BOGO Arabian colts
updated their profile picture.
June 19, 2015 · 🌐

Boost Unavailable

👍 Like   💬 Comment   ↪ Share

Jeanne Grunert, Katherine L. Kerr and 213 others   Chronological ▾

information. She hoped to squash most negativity from her precious boys' page before it even happened. Right off the bat, she knew people would squawk about the image that clearly showed Majus's extremely lax joints. And not to mention the fact that the situation of twins was "allowed" to happen in the first place. Jess shuddered at the possible negativity to come, but soldiered on and completed the fan page for the boys. Her stomach rumbled impatiently and the baby twitched in response, but Jess continued her work. She added albums of the sire and the dam as well as the videos from that morning's adventure outside.

Within hours, thousands of people had followed their page and, not surprisingly, several had already been ousted for negative comments.

Chapter Six

June 19th

Night

Deep gray clouds clung to the full moon, creating an ominous aura and a thick breeze slunk through the barn. The white mare was off grazing in the neighboring pasture with The Man's big chestnut gelding and The Boy's pony. She was growing increasingly uncomfortable, but was more or less patiently awaiting the completion of her stall. Having finished her hay, the black mare dozed in her stall while her magnificent bay filly slept soundly in the clean sawdust. In the roomy foaling stall, the chestnut mare munched her hay and gave her head a worried toss. Her udder was swelling uncomfortably full; the twins did not nurse well this evening. The golden colts slept deeply in the fresh bedding, dreaming of their brief afternoon romp. An ear twitch here, a tail flap there. The mare nuzzled her precious miracles and deep from the little one's belly rose a sinister rumbling. A few buzzards looped lazily above and perched upon the fencepost to observe.

Chapter Seven

June 20th- Morning

"Mom, what's wrong with the twins? They don't look so good," Aiden said as they stood in the stall giving the morning feed. Sweetie nickered impatiently from the field and Penny pawed next door at her stall mats. Flies, more flies than Jess realized occupied the farm, buzzed busily over the colts. They crawled eagerly across their weepy eyes and especially greedily on their damp, sticky rear ends. With shaking hands, Jess grabbed her phone, the vet clinic was closed. Of course it was closed, it was Saturday. She stifled a helpless whimper, sent a Facebook message to her vet, said a little prayer, and dialed again.

"Stephanie, are you working today?" Jess whispered in a panic over the phone. She wiped her mouth with her hand as she stared at the scene before her.

"No, what's the matter?" Stephanie asked in concern, hearing the tears threatening to overtake Jess's voice.

"The boys, they aren't nursing, they have diarrhea so *bad.* A few minutes ago, they tried to nurse some, but not much. Mona is so full, she's simply squirting milk all over herself. It's crusted all down her back legs. You have to get over here! They look terrible, they look, they look almost half-dead. My God, the flies!

They are everywhere, Steph! It's Saturday, the vets aren't open. I Facebooked Dr. Dayton, but I don't know when I will hear from her," Jess was fighting a losing battle with the tears that marched steadily down her cheeks.

"Jess, I'm on my way. Hang tight, see if you can find vet help," Stephanie said, already slipping into her dusty, brown Ariats.

Jess took a shaky breath and cringed as Majus's weak body convulsed again and another stream of dark, foul liquid shot out of his frail rear. With a sigh, he flopped into the deep, but no longer clean, bedding next to Majician, who simply twitched and squirted without even bothering to stand up. The flies buzzed excitedly and a new group gathered at the fresh wet spots.

Jess's phone rang and when she saw the number of her vet, she pounced.

"Jess. I got your message come out to the dog boutique down the road. I have some great paste that really soaks up the junk in their gut and firms everything back up again," offered Dr. Dayton.

"Thank you, as soon as I get the kids in the car, I'm on my way," Jess replied gratefully and sent a message to Stephanie letting her know where she would be.

Chapter Eight

June 20th- Afternoon

"Dr. Dayton," Jess pleaded into the phone, "it didn't work. They are worse. It's coming out clear now. It's like water. They won't even nurse at all. We've been milking Mona. They won't take her milk. They won't take the milk replacer I bought; they won't take the Karo syrup."

"Jess, I am about to leave for the weekend, give them one more dose and if they are not improving by about 7:00, call the emergency number. You must try to get some milk or milk replacer in them, you *must*," Dr. Dayton replied.

Stephanie and Jess tried their best. Neither colt would stand at this point, so the exhausted women worked as a team. One woman attempted to tilt a head up while the other force fed milk through a large syringe. Jess paused frequently to grab her large abdomen and grasp her knees while she caught her breath. She couldn't believe the pains *she* was getting across her own stomach, but she fought them. She told her body that the little chestnut lives in that stall depended on her and it would keep her own baby locked in place through this ordeal. The pains subsided and the women's' work continued.

Eventually, Jess and Steph were as exhausted as were the sick colts. Drops of milk spattered them from head to toe. Their hands were sticky with it and bits of bedding clung to the webbing of their fingers. Bits of bedding clung to their hair and their mournful faces reflected their dispirited souls. They trudged back to the house to check on the children and clean up.

Stephanie stayed as long as she could, both to support Jess and to help with the kids. Aiden was beside himself about the thought of losing the twins when they had just appeared to be so vital and healthy.

"It's not fair!" he shouted and retreated to his room where his boy tears would not be seen. *No,* he thought, *they're not going to sell these ones, these ones are just going to die.* And he buried his face deep into his pillow so no one would hear him sobbing as yet another piece of his tender heart broke off.

Chapter Nine

June 20th

Early Evening

Out in the barn, the twins' bellies bloated like two-day old August roadkill and the flies buzzed and buzzed and buzzed. The chestnut mare pawed uncomfortably; her udder felt as if it would explode. The Woman and her Friend had done an honest job of milking her, but as she was an excellent producer, the pressure was building again quickly. Her precious miracles refused to get up. She was aware that her people had tried to help them but it appeared as if they were unable to. Her colts were laying in the trampled straw and their lips pulled back from their gums in little grimaces of pain. A thick layer of black flies swarmed busily over their eyes, nostrils, exposed tongues and gums, and filthy rear ends. The colts' sick bodies trembled and they seemed to have lost at least ten precious pounds each in the course of that horrible day. Hip, rib, and shoulder bones protruded through dangerously dehydrated skin, threatening to slice their thin hides wide open. Their glassy eyes rolled back in their heads and the flies fed on.

The late afternoon sky began to darken prematurely as treacherous storm clouds marched in. Far in the distance, a long, low growl of thunder rolled ominously across the farmland and the mares looked nervously at the sky. More vultures were circling above, attracted by the death-smell wafting from the large stall.

Chapter Ten

June 20th

Night

"Hello? This is Jessica Williams. I have very sick foals, they are twins... two days old this morning.... Wha-what do you mean they will die and no one can come out ... How can you say that... But you haven't even looked at them!" The voice on the other end of the phone droned on with ridiculous excuses, but Jessica was numb to it. After speaking to two area vets who were not comfortable with working on the twins and no luck in getting a hold of anyone else, she dialed the local emergency number and waited. "Hello," she begged after the receptionist picked up, "please, who is the emergency on call vet tonight?"

"That would be Dr. Hanebutt, Ma'am," the receptionist responded. *This one sounds like a robot, too,* Jess thought as she nervously rubbed her belly, unconsciously feeling for a movement from her own baby within. *Doesn't anyone care?*

"Oh, thank goodness! Please, please can you have him call me?" The relief poured out of Jess. She knew Dr. Hanebutt would give an honest and thorough response as well as an explanation of his recommendations. "I have two day old twins and I think they are dying," Jess pleaded with the receptionist.

"What is the best number to reach you?" the robot voice inquired. "...Thank you, he will give you a call shortly."

Jessica dialed her mother while she waited for the call from the veterinarian. "Mom, hi, I hate to do this to you, but I need you to come out here. I know we talked earlier and I told you the twins are really sick. But, Mom, I think they are dying. I am waiting for Dr. Hanebutt to call back. I, I think I will need you to watch Aiden and Kat," she stammered.

"Oh, honey," Janine said, "I am already on my way."

The phone rang an agonizing five minutes later as the first fat raindrops exploded against the windows and the roof. Dr. Hanbutt patiently listened as Jess explained the downturn of the colts' health. After a brief analytical pause, he calmly responded. "Jess, you are going to have to take them to the New Bolton Center. Your colts need their blood work run immediately, and I don't have the labs on premise. I would not have results back from the state until Tuesday, and by then, I don't think they will still be with us. Let me call them and give you the referral. You should begin hooking your horse trailer up now." He hung up before she could hardly register, let alone argue how impossible that trip would be in her current state.

Jess's heart sank. A part of the University of Pennsylvania, New Bolton was the very best veterinary hospital around. It was eighty miles away and Matt had the newer Silverado. She would have to drive them in the farm truck in what was promising to be a very impressive summer storm. Jess hardly trusted that old truck to take her to the grocery store. And then, there would be the hospital fees. She didn't even want to think about how much this would set their farm back financially. Outside, a few giant raindrops slowly crashed to earth from the heavy thunderheads above.

*   *   *

As soon as Janine arrived, gave the already sleeping kids a quick kiss and headed out to hook up the horse trailer in the dark. Large raindrops splattered on Jess's head and rolled down her face as she bent over the hitch. They were falling at a steadily increasing frequency. Her belly bulged uncomfortably as she tried to bend over to hook the trailer. The beam of the flashlight Janine held in less than steady hands glowed pathetically in the thick dark night. Clumsy fingers fumbled at the slick metal and Jess cursed under her breath when a fingernail snapped at the quick and scarlet blood greedily filled the nail bed. She stood up and stretched her uncomfortable back and Janine finally spoke her concern.

"How are we going to get them loaded?"

"Well, mom, I don't think they'll run away." Jess realized her response was unnecessarily snarky and softened her tone. "I'm guessing that I can get Mona on the trailer and you can just kind of lift them in. I don't think they weigh much more than a bag of grain at this point." She pushed her damp bangs from her face and took a shaky breath.

"Ok," Janine said, doubtful of her capabilities, but knowing her daughter needed her. "Let's do this."

Jess started the old two-toned Silverado, which was well on its way to racking up a quarter of a million miles. It faithfully roared to life and she slid onto the well-worn driver's seat with her large belly pressing uncomfortably against the steering wheel. She fidgeted with the seat, but found that when she slid it far enough back to make room for her pregnant stomach, her feet wouldn't reach the pedals. *Figures,* she thought, *this will be an uncomfortable ride.* She drove the truck around to the barn and threw it in park as the rainfall increased. Mona watched from over her stall door with trepidation.

"Hey, girl," Jess addressed the chestnut mare with a shaky voice. Trembling hands slipped the old, red halter onto Mona's patient head. She tenderly patted the mare's sleek neck. "I need you to be good, Mo. I'm trying to help your babies. You need to be careful on this trailer ride and not step on your boys." Mona nosed her arm nervously, sensing Jess's apprehension. "Ok, Mom, let's go," Jess said firmly over her shoulder.

Jennifer Wilson

Janine was able to coax the twins to a standing position once Jess led Mona out of the stall and she guided them toward the trailer. Mona nickered and stomped her feet impatiently as her colts weakly stumbled their way to her in the dark. Once all three horses were gathered at the rear of the open-stall stock trailer, Jess led Mona on. Immediately, Mona spun around inside the trailer and pinned her against the wall. Jess instinctively sucked her stomach in as far as possible, turned sideways, and threw her shoulder into that of the panicking mare's. "Easy, girl!" Jess soothed as Mona pressed her ever tighter against the wall and strained against the lead, "Mom, get them in here!"

The rain was now coming down steadily and the sick, confused colts milled around at the trailer door, neither strong enough nor certain how to step up and join their mother inside. With the rain pouring down her face, Janine wrapped her arms around Majus's slick chest and stinking rear and heaved him inside. Mona shoved Jess roughly to the side and with a maternal nicker, nuzzled her colt to reassure both him and herself. Meanwhile, Janine repeated the process with Majician. In a scramble of legs, both colts were loaded, shivering from fever and rain. Jess snapped the tie to Mona's halter, kissed her soft muzzle and reminded her one more time to be careful.

"Jess, *you* be careful," Janine pleaded. "This is terrible weather. You shouldn't be doing this. You are my daughter and that is my granddaughter you are carrying; take care of everyone and call me when you get there, no matter how late." The women exchanged a brief hug and then Jess was in the truck and pulling out of the driveway in the dark, rainy night.

Sweet Rose, the senior broodmare, was kicking in discomfort at her own swollen belly and udder out in the back pasture as the pouring rain increased. With a deep groan, she laid down under the trees edging the pasture.

Chapter Eleven

June 20th-21st

It was nearly 10:30 p.m. when the old truck crept out of the driveway in the streaming rain. The windshield wipers swished back and forth but they made a strange whirring noise. The truck stopped at the intersection but the brakes squealed in angry protest. The truck faithfully accelerated but it was slow and laborious. *Please, God. Please let us make it. Don't leave me stranded with these dying miracles on the side of the highway in the pouring rain. Please...* The cell phone screamed in the dark cab and yanked Jess out of her desperate prayers. It was the vet from New Bolton Center, Dr. Linton. Her voice was soft and gentle, soothing and calm in Jess's time of worry and despair.

"Good evening, Mrs. Williams. I am Dr. Linton, and I will be taking care of your very special boys. Are you able to talk? Can you give me background information- from the breeding to the foaling and what has transpired over the last twenty-four hours? We want to be ready for them as soon as you arrive."

Jess spilled the entire story in great relief as the miles rolled away under the almost-but-not-quite-bald tires of the two-tone blue Silverado and the steady rain turned into a downpour.

Twenty-five miles into the eighty-mile voyage, the windshield wipers stopped.

*   *   *

Dear God! Jess thought in panic as the water immediately pooled on the vertical windshield of the ancient truck and began flowing upwards as the wind turned the water into currents. Jess desperately strained to see through the shifting kaleidoscope of colors and distorted images. Her speed fell back to thirty miles per hour, then down to twenty-five miles per hour. Jess had a few brief miles to thank her stars that it was late at night and that she would not likely encounter much traffic before she registered that several sets of headlights were coming toward her in the south-bound lane. Far too many lights for this time of night. The several lights appeared to become a steady stream of vehicles heading south. The head lights refracted in the water running up the windshield, distorting her visibility even further and making it all but impossible for Jess to see. She steadied her route by fixating her vision on the highway's white shoulder line. To her ever increasing horror, a few more miles north and she saw a billion red taillights glaring menacingly just ahead of her.

What the heck is this? She thought in amazement. *There is no way there should be this much traffic! What is happening?*

Jennifer Wilson

Like the proverbial ton of bricks, it hit her. This weekend was the Firefly Festival, a huge weekend-long music celebration much like a modern-day Woodstock. At first she couldn't understand why so many people would be leaving on Saturday at almost midnight. Then flashing orange added to the visual confusion and eventually what appeared to be lights from several state police vehicles. Her confused brain finally registered- they must have evacuated the festival because of the storm. All 65,000 music fanatics leaving at the same time; most certainly not having planned on driving any time soon. As if in response, a wicked streak of lightning split the sky, momentarily blinding her. Within another mile, she was engulfed in traffic speeding past her over twenty miles per hour faster than her pathetic snail's crawl. She heaved a great breath, fought back the tears and fumbled for the hazard lights switch. Vehicle after vehicle whipped past her, throwing up more water on her windshield, further complicating her visual impairment. Finally, certain that she would vomit, Jess pulled off onto the shoulder of the highway. Without the wind to shove the rain in torrents up the windshield, the visibility cleared considerably. Jess spent a few minutes regaining her confidence, inhaled deeply and waited for a break in traffic. She eased the ancient truck and rusty trailer back onto the highway and almost immediately her windshield again became a fury of mini rivers flowing relentlessly up and shattering visibility.

Majus and Majician - The BOGO Arabian colts

June 21, 2015 ·

[Like Page]

The boys are now at New Bolton. Prognosis is pretty good, but they will be there at least 5 days. The vet says they are amazing, strong and vital. They have some sort of bacterial infection that they are treating with dual antibiotics. Mona is being mother of the year and giving Arabians a good name! They quoted about $5,000 for the vet bill... We could certainly use a little help for that! Even just a dollar or two adds up to get the best care for these guys possible - the... See More

Click here to support The boys' New Bolton fund by Jennifer Baker Wilson

Majician and Majus are extremely rare identical twins. They were also unexpected as they were from a single placenta and showed as a single embryo spot on the...

GOFUNDME.COM

14,902 people reached

[Boost Post]

Jennifer Wilson

And so she proceeded, crawling along between twenty to twenty-five miles per hour, pulling over every time her nerves threatened to explode. Jess had no idea what was going on in the trailer behind her; she could only pray that Mona was maintaining herself back there and not stepping on her very sick, very fragile, and very precious cargo.

*   *   *

Forty miles and an hour and a half later, Jess was in Northern Delaware. Not as secure with this area as Route 1, she had to rely on her GPS to show her just how close she was to the I-95 North split. By this time, traffic had thinned out again and, thankfully, she was mostly on her own as she crawled blindly up the highway, desperately trying to read the exit signs and putting her faith in the accuracy of her GPS. What seemed like a century later, she found herself on Newark Rd., searching for the dreaded sharp turn onto 926. Her GPS insisted that it was immediately ahead of her, but she could not see it at all. She limped along the shoulder, straining for a glimpse of something in the horribly lit road. *Come on,* she thought, *I am only a couple of miles away!* She grumbled under her breath as she saw the turn to 926 slide by and she bounced into a pothole along the shoulder. It took her another 6 miles round trip to get back to the site of that dreadful turn. *How in the world do people with larger horse trailers do this? Please, PLEASE, I still can't see it!* Although the rain had slowed to an easy but steady shower, lights still refracted wildly off the wet windshield, distorting her vision and making it nearly impossible to see the dark, treacherous turn. *PLEASE, I need help!* In an answer to her desperate pleading, the windshield wipers that had shorted out over two hours before came back to life. With a clear sight, Jess was able to navigate the sharp turn and the windy Street Road with ease. Five minutes later, she stopped in the center of the nearly empty New Bolton parking lot, put the truck in park, crossed her arms over her belly, dropped her head on the steering wheel and cried.

Her great sobs of relief were interrupted by a gentle knock at the window. The lady who greeted Jess kindly showed her inside where she filled out the mountains of admissions paperwork prior to unloading her sick colts. Finally, the staff was ready to welcome the boys, who were sleeping, but safe, in the trailer. Jess grabbed the lead line and stepped toward the trailer to unload Mona, but a staff member softly put a hand on her tired arm. "We have them," she said with a gentle smile.

Jess watched in amazement as more staff members appeared, covered head to toe in white suits, gloves, masks, and covered boots. To her, they appeared to be scientists ready for work in a Level 4 Biohazard laboratory. There was one for each twin and the mare and together, the team escorted them through a garage door into the Neonatal Intensive Care Unit. Before Jess could round the corner to kiss them good luck, the door was closed. She didn't even get the opportunity to tell her babies goodbye. She wondered if she would ever see them again.

*　　*　　*

The rain had long since ended, and Jess experienced a far more relaxing ride home. She pulled into the driveway around 4:00 am, woke her mother, and briefly explained the epic journey. Then, she collapsed into her empty bed, curled up in a ball with her arms cradling her belly, and slept.

Chapter Twelve

June 21st

Meanwhile, eighty miles away, the chestnut mare nervously watched as strangers in strange clothing swarmed over her colts. She was comfortable in a well bedded, padded stall, but there was equipment everywhere. Before long, vials of blood were being drawn and rushed out for analysis. IVs were inserted and attached to the ceiling on long, spiraling tubes to keep them out of the way of long necks and long legs. The mare was also stuck with a needle for some reason, but she tolerated the procedure. She was very aware that her boys were dangerously ill and some maternal instinct in her understood that that these strange humans were trying to help. She was even quiet when they came in and separated her fading colts from both her and each other.

Jennifer Wilson

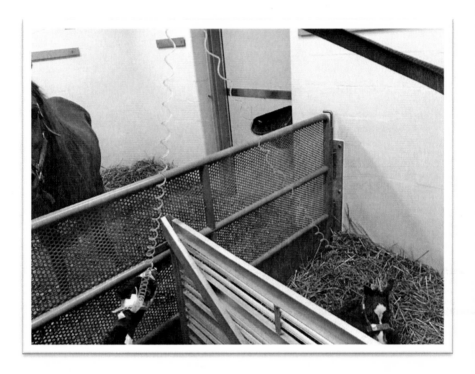

Chapter Thirteen

June 21st- Morning

The boisterous crowing of their rooster roused Jess from her slumber a mere three hours later; she groggily drug herself out of her bed and trudged out to feed the horses. The summer breeze, crisp and fresh from the night's cleansing, playfully shook the leaves in the trees as she wandered down the path toward the farm. Birds sang while squirrels skittered through the underbrush. The peaceful atmosphere combined with her utter exhaustion placed her in a trance-like state and she didn't notice that The Sweet Rose addressed her breakfast with only mild interest.

Inside, Janine had the kids up and eating. She noticed with eternal gratitude that dishes were done and the kitchen was sparkling.

"Mommy!!!!" Jess was greeted with the pure joy that only children between the ages of two and four can muster. Aiden's mouth smiled, but his typically bright eyes were dimmed with concern for his mother and the foals. Although he was young, he was well aware that she was doing far more than a mother as far along in pregnancy as she was should have been doing. He had seen foals born every year of his life and knew how pampered the mares were towards the end of their term. His mother treated them like queens, but she was running herself ragged. He naturally found his three year old sister quite annoying; nevertheless, he was crazy excited about his new sister who was due in just over two more months.

"How are they, Mommy?" Aiden asked in deep concern.

Jess poured herself a small bowl of cereal and thought for a moment before responding. "They arrived alive and the vets immediately began working on them." She poured the milk and shut the refrigerator door quietly. "I believe they are still ok right now, or else we would have received a phone call."

An hour later, Janine packed her bags to return home and gave her daughter a supportive hug.

"They will be strong, they have a wonderful mother and many people sending out strong prayers for them."

"I hope so, Mom. They looked so good. They are too amazing to lose now."

"I know. Please, call me the moment you hear any word. Are you sure you don't need me to stay until Matt gets home?"

"I will mom. And I'm good. I feel fine. He won't be too late with all that's going on, and Aiden will help take care of Kat. Your kitties miss you and you have to work tomorrow. You need *your* rest too! I love you"

"I love you, too," Janine gave her daughter another warm hug, kissed her forehead and turned to head home.

Less than satisfied with the vague response his mother gave him that morning, Aiden finished his breakfast and sulked out to the barn where his dark, dappled grey pony, Cosmo, nickered a warm greeting and then promptly presented his rump for a good scratch. Normally, a silly rump scratch request from his pony was all it took to cheer him up. Today, he needed more. He travelled across to the adjoining pasture and let himself in to see Penny and her new filly, Cali. Cali, full of foal curiosity, ambled right up and chewed on his tee-shirt. She dropped his damp shirt and stretched her long neck out to sniff his nose. Feathery foal whiskers tickled his face and, finally, he smiled. He breathed in her sweet scent of milk and grass and hay and buried his fingers in her soft baby coat.

"Hey, girl. You sure are a sweet thing." Aiden loved this filly, but remained guarded. "Mommy says you aren't for sale. She says we have enough land now and that you and Sweetie's baby this summer are keepers. But I don't know that I can believe that." Cali rubbed her tiny, velvet muzzle on his forehead, eliciting a giggle. "There just has to be a way."

*   *   *

In the house, Jess was thinking the exact same thing. *There just has to be a way.* Not only was she guaranteed that her plans of

81

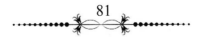

using the funds of Mona's *filly* to support the expansion of the farm, she was now guaranteed of being several additional thousands of dollars in the hole. She would do everything she could to pay New Bolton whatever it took to keep them alive but reality was staring her in her face harder than her dreamer soul preferred. This was not just a step or two back, this was leaps and leaps back. She posted the sad news of the sick twins on Facebook and requested prayers. Many concerned friends sent her private messages regarding the cost of sending the precious twins to New Bolton. Considering more than one suggestion given by her online friends and supporters, Jess called her mother for a conformation.

"Hey, Mom."

"Hi, honey! How are the boys?" Janine asked anxiously.

"I don't know; I haven't heard yet. I am going to assume in this situation that no call generally means they are at least still alive."

Janine agreed.

"Mom, I have to ask your opinion on something."

"What's that, honey?"

"Well, I can't even begin to imagine how much this will cost. And, well, some of my Facebook friends think I should accept donations. There are people out there who really *want* to help. It feels awkward though." Although Jess was always a giver and made donations to many charities and organizations over the years, she felt strange accepting donations for medical costs that were incurred by her own personal horses.

"Oh, honey. Well, if people want to help, I think you should consider it. I don't think this is a time to be prideful."

"I know. I know." Jess sighed. She wasn't sure if she was feeling a butterfly for baby flutter inside.

After a few more minutes of discussion, the women hung up and, with some hesitation, Jess began to set up a GoFundMe account. Hours later, as expected, she had received some very nasty and uncalled for private messages. The offenders were blocked and she fought back the tears. Not as expected, more donations that she could have imagined were flooding into her new account.

Chapter Fourteen

June 21st- Afternoon

The old grey broodmare swished her long, thick tail, tips deeply yellowed from her time outside, and stood in the delicious shade gifted by the woods at the edge of the pasture. She was grateful for her fly sheet, for the horseflies were voracious this time of year. They bred rampantly in the nearby wetlands. Over the past few days, she had not received much attention from her people. This was strange, as typically when she was so close to her time, The Woman practically swarmed over her. The Woman would brush her, bathe her, pamper her, and loiter in her stall for hours. She would come and check on her throughout the night every couple of hours for nights on end.

Now, she had been uncomfortable for three days and she could feel the foal was in position. Her udder was heavy and waxed and the droplets had turned from golden amber to milky white this morning. And still, The Woman had not noticed. This was not the first time they were pregnant together; eight years earlier they both carried their first Sons. The Woman had given birth to The Boy and the old grey mare, then young and glowing, had given birth to the great grey gelding whose soul was kind but full of fire. Even then, in her own discomfort, The Woman had paid great attention to her. The old mare did not understand why this time was different. A hard contraction shivered down her flank and her white shoulder turned dark with sweat in the bright summer afternoon.

Chapter Fifteen

June 21 Night

Jess was exhausted. She dragged through her day in a hazy dream, allowing her children to indulge in as many cartoons, snacks, and candies as their little hearts desired. When he walked in the door, Matt saw how exhausted his expecting wife was and he instructed her to take a shower while he fed the horses their evening meals. Thinking only of getting back to the house to tend for his wife, he did not think to check The Sweet Rose; she was not due for nearly two more weeks. He did not notice that she merely gazed after him when he poured her grain in the big tub in the back pasture and strode toward the house to care for Jess.

"Jess, you really need to go to sleep," Matt pleaded.

"I can't, I'm waiting for the vet to call. I haven't heard from her at all yet. I just don't understand why she didn't call yet. They must be ok."

On cue, the phone rang.

"Hello?" Jess whimpered, terrified to answer.

"Hello! Is this Jessica?" Dr. Linton's voice was calm, yet empathetic.

"Yes, how are the boys?"

"They are doing ok. We have had to separate them from the mare. They have nasty bacteria in their blood. We can't say from where they got it, so we have to look at all factors. We will milk the mare to keep her producing, but we need to eliminate her as a possibility."

"You mean she could have made them sick? This might not have anything to do with them being twins?" Jess asked in disbelief.

"This more or less does not have to do with them being twins. The bacteria probably hit their systems harder than it would a single foal because they were smaller in size than normal foals at birth. But really," Dr. Linton mused, "their similarity in size is incredible; most of the time with a twinning, one is considerably smaller than the other. These two are really remarkable, and so handsome." The admiration in the vet's voice made Jess smile despite the grave situation.

"So, will they be ok?"

"We can't be sure yet. They are eating from the bottle and their fluids are better. They have a long way to go; they were very, very sick little boys. I can't make any promises right now. We have them all separated from each other with stall dividers, but Mona can touch them and nose them over the dividers. I will send you some pictures tonight when my shift is over and will call again in the morning when we make the next run of blood work." Jess could hear the genuine concern in Dr. Linton's gentle voice. "Now, we need to discuss your budget. I am sorry, but this is likely to get very expensive."

A jolt ran through her body and her breath caught in her chest. Jessica was not looking forward to facing the reality of what keeping these little guys alive would be; she already had enough into their breeding as last summer was cool and cloudy and their dam, like many mares across the country that season, was reluctant to come into heat.

"How much do you think this will cost? I mean, if you could give me an estimate? Just a ballpark?" Jess was unaware of the little sliver of skin she had nervously worked off the surface of her lip as she chewed anxiously.

"I really think they will need to be here at least throughout the week. We need to monitor their blood work twice a day and ensure the counts are getting to a normal, healthy level. I would estimate that the six-to-seven days' board, medications, lab fees and blood analysis will probably put you around the $5,000 range," Dr. Linton honestly reported.

The butterfly in Jess's stomach leaped to her spine and fluttered up her back. Dr. Linton's figure was what she was expecting, but not what she wanted to hear.

The stodgy little accountant in the dusty corner of her brain who kept track of all of her ridiculous horse expenses shoved her horn-rimmed glasses up her nose and began banging on her tiny calculator at light speed. *First, this breeding cost more than anticipated as Mona took forever to come in heat. Next, you just moved. The barn isn't even DONE! Actually, it isn't even a barn... it's a fancy open front shed. More like a run-in on steroids. You have sixteen acres... only about three are even fenced. Did I say sixteen acres? You own eleven... you actually need to BUY the last five from your patient brother-in-law. You need to plant and fence in about ten more acres. What are you going to plant them with? You need a mower. You don't even have a LAWN MOWER for the beautiful yard you just bought. And your vehicles! What a mess! They all have over 200,000 miles on them. Did you forget you are pregnant? How could you forget that??? You need a new-to-you vehicle to hold a family of five; you will not get three kids around in that dinky, two-door Alero. Yes, you have money in the bank thanks to the sale of your smaller home.... but it's dwindling quickly. It's NOT FOR THE HORSES!*

"Thank you, thank you for everything. We can go up to five thousand dollars. Please let me know right away if it will require more."

The little accountant in her brain slammed her head on her desk and a wisp of silver hair slipped out of her prim bun.

*　　*　　*

Out in the back field, The Sweet Rose had not eaten a speck of her evening grain. She was racked with contractions and dripping with sweat. With a heavy groan, she sank to her knees and despite the discomfort of the fly sheet that clung to her soaking wet body she rolled to her side and began to push.

Chapter Sixteen

June 22

Early Morning

The early morning summer sun glowed lovingly on the exquisite bay colt that lay in slumber at the edge of the back pasture. Although he was nearly two weeks early, he was huge and well filled out; he looked like a two week old foal. Because he was a summer foal, his baby coat was sleek and glittered in the morning light. The old grey mare nuzzled him with concern. Although he was born many hours ago, he had not yet nursed successfully. The fly sheet, which did its job in deterring the wicked variety of horseflies that plagued the farm in the summer, made it impossible for the newborn colt to figure out how to nurse.

He was hungry, and instinct told him that his mother would nourish him. Instinct directed him to her full udder. But instinct was not prepared to handle the confusing tangle of a sheet draped over his dam, blocking his direct route to the nourishment. Several times he got up and attempted in vain to find the rich milk his body desperately needed. The old grey mare waited patiently and nickered in encouragement but he simply couldn't. He was weakening; his naps grew longer and his attempts to nurse grew shorter. In the golden rays of the warming sun, he slept again.

Chapter Seventeen

June 22

Mid Morning

Jess awakened just before seven that morning, feeling delightfully refreshed from her solid night's sleep. She yawned and stretched and heard Matt rustling in the kitchen down stairs as he was getting ready for work. Pulling her light robe around her, she wandered downstairs.

What a glorious morning, she thought as she descended the steps. Although the situation with the twins remained serious, the very tired, very pregnant part of her was grateful their care was in the hands of experts for a while. She was secretly even grateful they were far enough away that she would not be tempted to visit; there remained boxes to unpack from their move barely a month ago and the horses at home needed some attention. Also, she desperately needed time to recuperate- from the long school year, the sudden move, and the chaos that had comprised the previous few days.

"Good morning, beautiful," Matt greeted her with a kiss. He handed her a fragrant, steaming mug, her half-cup of coffee in which she indulged every few days. "What an incredible morning!"

Jess closed her eyes and breathed deep the comforting aroma of the coffee. She moseyed on out to the corner rocking chair that was positioned near the gigantic plate glass window in the living room and she gazed out at the birds and butterflies dancing in the branches outside. Matt kissed her forehead and left for work. There she rocked, contentedly sipping her coffee and playing a little Candy Crush for nearly two hours.

Finally, feeling more than a little guilty that the horses had waited far too late for their morning feed, Jess motivated herself to get dressed. She poked her head into Aiden's room and saw the kids were still sound asleep in his bunk bed; the adventurous Kat was on the top bunk and Aiden was breathing deeply on the bottom. She slipped downstairs, tied up her boots and quietly shut the back door behind her.

Outside, it was a divine summer morning. Devoid of humidity, the air was warm and fresh. Jess felt near euphoria as she sauntered down the winding woods path that led to the old cattle barn at the back of the farm. She breathed in the clean air, gently caressed her growing belly and reveled in the perfection of the day. Today, she would bathe Sweetie and polish her to a glowing white in preparation for her upcoming arrival. Jess would braid her mane, whiten her yellow tail, and maybe even dig around the boxes and tubs in the barn and unpack the clippers. The lovely lady could use some trimming up around her ankles and ears as she would soon be the subject matter of many pictures and videos. Tonight, her wonderful husband would lay down the mats in the final stall and the shed-style barn would be complete. It would be ready to welcome the arrival of their final foal this year.

By the time Jess got to the barn, her face was in a wide grin. However, the blissful smile fled her face as she realized that Sweetie was not at the front gate, pacing, pawing and loudly demanding her breakfast. Rather, she was standing along the woods line at the back of the pasture, looking at Jess, then sniffing the long grass in front of her, then looking at Jess again before returning her attention to the grass in front of her.

No. No you didn't!

On adrenaline-weak legs, she gasped a weak breath and made her way across the pasture to the treasured mare who was not due to foal for two more weeks. Although every thread of her being rejected the thought of Sweetie foaling outside in a fly sheet, Jess knew the mare inside out and was well aware of what she was walking towards. *Please let it be ok. Please let her be ok!*

As Jess approached the mare, she could make out a rich, bay body lying in the grass. Please be just sleeping… my gosh, that thing looks huge! Is that a perfect diamond I see? I wonder if this will stay bay or turn grey…. that is too pretty of a marking to be swallowed up by a grey coat. Please be a filly, please. Please be ok. Jess's mind was a jumble of thoughts as she approached her

Jennifer Wilson

last foal of the season. Upon reaching the two horses, she could just faintly see the foal's rib cage rising and falling with soft breaths. Sweetie nervously nosed the foal and peered at Jess. She was an excellent mother, but was always edgy for the first forty-eight hours.

"Easy Mamma. Let's get this fly sheet off of you," Jess murmured to the watchful mare. Sweet Rose stood steady as Jess first unbuckled the leg straps, then the belly strap and finally, the chest straps. Calmly and gently she grasped the blanket at the wither and tail and eased it off. She slowly backed away from Sweetie so as not to startle her.

"I'll be right back with some breakfast, lady. You must be starving."

Sweetie eyed her and then sniffed her sleeping baby again.

Momentarily, Jess returned with a halter, a feed tub and a small portion of grain. "Here you go, Sweetie," Jess soothed as she slipped on the mare's black halter. "You know the drill, you can get your full amount when you poo. Unfortunately, you did this in the pasture and I have no way of telling if you have gone yet. What were you thinking?" Jess scowled.

Sweetie happily scarfed up the few handfuls of grain, then returned her attentions to the still sleeping foal. With Sweetie taken care of, Jess pulled out her phone and snapped a few quick, obligatory shots and then dialed Matt.

"Hi, honey… I need you to come home," Jess whispered into the phone. "Sweetie had her baby last night. "

"You're kidding me," Matt responded incredulously. "She was outside!"

"Yeah, I know."

"Is the baby ok? Is it a colt or filly?"

"I don't know either. It's sleeping. Hang on." Jess squatted down with her giant belly uncomfortably squeezed between her knees and balanced herself. Once steady, she ran a gentle hand down the foal's feather-soft coat and gently lifted the tail, craning her neck and wobbling on the balls of her toes.

"It's a colt."

"You're kidding," Matt said for the second time in as many minutes.

"Nope. But, man, he's gorgeous. I'll send a pic."

"Ok, I'll be home as quickly as possible. Be careful. Love you."

"Love you, too."

Jess texted the pictures to Stephanie, no words needed, and then proceeded to wake the sleeping baby and see if he would nurse. Like a flash the giant colt was up and hiding behind his mother. *This will be fun,* Jess mused sarcastically; there was little she hated worse than a foal that missed being imprinted. She knew that combined with being pregnant it would make this one next to impossible to train. She had missed the first golden hours of contact and Sweetie's babies were generally standoffish in the beginning to begin with.

WHAT THE HECK!!! Steph's text buzzed in Jess's pocket and Jess giggled at the excitement and disbelief in the capital letters in spite of the situation.

Can you come out today? I can't do this alone. Don't know when Matt will get home.

On my way!!!

Jess observed with dismay as the colt clumsily fumbled around his mother's flank, chest and udder. He licked. He sucked. He nibbled. He did not latch. He looked good now, but the clock was ticking on getting his colostrum, that priceless first milk that held all of the antibodies his newborn immune system needed to survive in the outside world. Jess was also painfully aware that he had been born who-knew-how-many hours ago and that his umbilical stump had not been treated with iodine. Despite the heavy risk of septic infection, she'd have to wait until assistance arrived. In no way was she going to attempt to cleanse his stump fat and pregnant in the middle of a field with a colt who looked to be at least two weeks old and full of muscle. Exhausted and defeated, the starving colt flopped weakly back into the deep summer grass and closed his eyes.

Jess checked the time. She had just a few minutes to call her mother to report the news before Janine headed to work, then she would call Dr. Dayton and have her come out to perform the new foal checkup and the blood work.

Chapter Eighteen

June 22

Late Morning

Stephanie arrived within an hour. Jess spent that time walking the pasture with an old, empty bucket, searching desperately for the placenta. Thus far, she had only found two small pieces; it appeared some scavenger had found it and eaten some of it and maybe drug the rest off elsewhere.

"Let's do the umbilical cord," Jess said after greeting her friend with a weary hug.

"Absolutely," Stephanie agreed.

The colt was sleeping again, and Stephanie was able to get in a good soaking before he awoke, leaped to his feet and scuttled around the other side of his mother. Jess thanked the Lord that Sweetie was a mare who would not walk away because they were still out in the pasture.

"Ugh... I don't know, Jess," Steph muttered in a disgusted voice. "His stump is all dried up and crispy. I don't know that iodine did any good." Her face crinkled.

"Well, we tried. We will have to keep our fingers crossed. Let's get him eating; he hasn't nursed at all yet."

"All right, dumb-dumb," Stephanie chuckled. "Let's get you eating."

She boldly slipped around the mare and deftly hooked her arms around the chest and rear of the giant colt before he could escape. She gently scratched with her long fingers while she held tight and reassured him until he relaxed. Then she guided him from Sweetie's front legs to her rear legs. With one hand steadying his rear, she reached under Sweetie's belly with the other hand and squeezed a bit of milk onto her fingers. She rubbed the liquid gold on his seeking gums. Immediately, the colt threw his head up in sheer excitement, lost his balance, and crashed to the ground.

"Get up!" Steph lifted the clumsy colt back to his feet and tried again. Every time he got a drop of milk in his mouth, he would stumble backward in excitement, lose his balance, and fall down. After about half an hour, everyone was tiring. "He's so big, he has to bend way down and really twist his neck to latch on," Stephanie observed. "He just can't balance like that yet. And he's really getting tired."

Jess loathed the idea of bottle feeding him as it could make him a very lazy nurser. However, he needed nutrition, and time was running short.

"Let me get the big dosing syringe we used on the twins. It's up at the house, and I need to wash it first. Let's let him rest a while."

The two women trekked back through the woods to the house, located the syringe and thoroughly washed it with scalding hot water and soap. While there, they checked on Aiden and Kat. Evidence on the kitchen table informed the ladies that Aiden had made himself and his sister peanut butter and jelly sandwiches at some point, complete with two cups of milk. Now, Aiden was watching Sponge Bob while Kat was working feverishly on her latest piece of three-year-old art. Jess took a moment to say a prayer of thanks that her children were so self-sufficient.

"What's up, Mom? Where have you been?" Aiden implored.

"Sweetie had her baby last night. A colt. He's having trouble nursing. Steph is helping out until Daddy can get home."

"Yes!!!" Aiden squealed in joy. "I'm going out to see him!"

"No, Honey, let us get him nursing first. It is really bad that he hasn't eaten yet. We will come get you once he's all good. Please keep an eye on Kat for me until I come get you." Aiden sullenly agreed to continued babysitter duty.

Back in the pasture, Stephanie milked the patient Sweetie into the large bottle manufactured for cattle and other stock animals and carefully poured some of the milk into the syringe.

"How do you want to do this," she asked Jess.

"Well, he needs to eat. But I don't want him to get lazy. Do you think I could try to steady him and you could get on the other side with the syringe and then when he tries to find the teat, you can squirt the syringe in his mouth? Maybe this way, he will know he has to reach under her to get it, but he will get something so he will stop giving up?" Jess suggested her plan hopefully, but with a hint of doubt in her voice.

Stephanie nodded, "Sounds good to me."

Together, the two women worked once again as a team. "Make sure you are ready for him to rock back hard when he gets it," Stephanie cautioned. "He's strong as an ox!"

"Gotcha," Jess nodded.

Once they had him in position, the hungry colt again attempted to nurse from his patient dam. This time, when his mouth began searching, Stephanie, hunkered down on the other side of the mare, stuck the syringe in his mouth and squirted. As anticipated, he rocked back hard in surprise and excitement. Jess held fast and stifled a cry of pain as he slammed into her abdomen. She planted her heels and shoved his weight forward, where he began searching for the nourishment again. By the time the syringe was empty, he was ready for more and eager to suckle. Stephanie shoved an engorged teat, dripping milk, into his toothless mouth. He latched and greedily suckled. Brilliant droplets of milk twinkled on his whiskers and once done, he contentedly sucked on his tongue and laid down with a very full belly. The women collapsed in the deep grass and laughed, sharing a satisfied smile.

"You know," Stephanie said, "he's simply gorgeous."

"I know," Jess breathed, resting one hand on her stomach and feeling the baby give a few kicks.

"Like better than Maghnus, maybe, just gorgeous."

"Yeah, I know."

"Do you think he will turn grey?"

"No, I am pretty sure this one is bay."

They smiled in the bright sunlight and delighted in the slice of heaven before them before they headed back to the house to gather the kids so they could meet the newest member of the family.

Chapter Nineteen

June 22nd-June 29th

It was a surreal week for Jessica. She was exhausted; but there was so much more to do. She lived through her days like a daze, anxiously awaiting each call from Dr. Linton. For the first few days, the colts' prognosis fluctuated. They would look good for several hours, then they would backslide again as their tiny bodies fought the persistent bacteria. With the care of the New Bolton Staff, however, they gradually showed increasing improvement.

With the love of the warm summer sun and the nourishment of their mothers, Cali and the new bay colt, named Majestik, played and flourished. Jessica took this blissfully calm week to relax and simply admire the beautiful creations with which her Half Arabian mares had blessed her. She spent many hours simply sitting in a lawn chair out in the pasture watching the foals frolic along with Aiden while Kat played contentedly in the dirt pile. Majestik, Jesse for short, was a large, bold colt. Although Cali was a good-sized filly and older, it was evident he would soon surpass her in size. Jessica could already envision the National Champion rose garlands encircling their necks and could see Aiden develop as a successful youth handler and rider with horses of this quality to show. Would these finally be the babies she would take to the glamorous Scottsdale show herself? Gazing at these works of art, the possibilities were endless to her.

Amidst her daydreaming and National Champion staring, somewhere in the far corner of Jessica's mind, the little accountant nagged her that Mona was *supposed* to produce a filly. A filly worthy of fetching a nice price in the overseas market. Maybe even a filly nice enough that they could sell Mona *and* the filly in a sweet package deal. Those were the sales that would make training and showing the Half Arabian foals possible. The stodgy old lady reiterated that in no way would Jess be able to keep the Half Arab foals and the miracle twins and buy more acreage and build a large, proper barn. For the time-being, Jess ignored the admonishments and lived the dream.

Jennifer Wilson

Jennifer Wilson

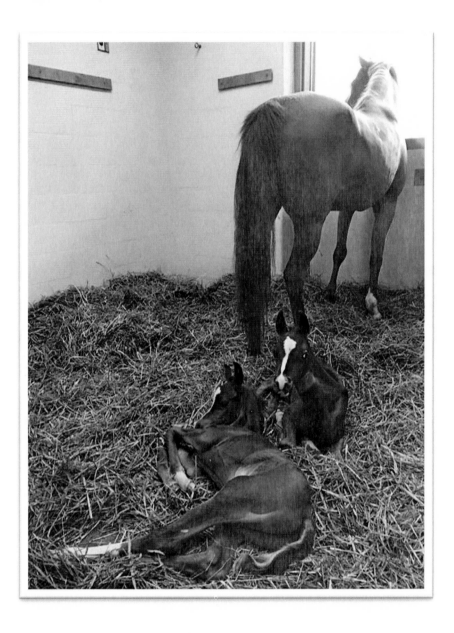

Chapter Twenty

June 29th

"Good morning, Jess," Dr. Linton's voice was bright and cheerful. "This morning's blood work came back great, I think it is safe for you to take the boys home. We will miss them very much- they have become regular little celebrities around here!"

Jess's heart fluttered happily. The twins were healthy again, and they would soon be back home. She wondered how much they had grown and if they were truly as beautiful as she remembered. Dr. Linton went over some final instructions, including additional blood work in the next 5 days to ensure their delicate blood counts continued to normalize.

Jess shot a text to Stephanie to let her know they were ready to go. She passed the time waiting for Stephanie by stripping down the foaling stall and spraying every surface with a bleach water mix. She then thoroughly swept out the rusty, but faithful, horse trailer and hosed it down while Aiden and Kat played on their favorite dirt pile in the horse pasture. Once it was mostly dry, she also sprayed the inside walls and floor mats of the trailer with the bleach mixture.

Matt had taken the old farm truck to work in anticipation of the twins' homecoming. Upon Stephanie's arrival, Aiden and Kat

were packed into the much-more-comfortable crew cab Silverado and the happy group of four headed out into the bright sunshine. Jess happily tapped her fingers on her stomach and mused over how different this trip was from the one made barely over a week before. Day versus night; hope versus dread; crystal blue sky versus ominous black storm clouds.

The trip to Kennett Square, Pennsylvania was fairly quick and without incident. Once at the great equine hospital, Stephanie kept watch over the kids while Jessica settled up with the billing department. Her delicate hands trembled as she wrote out the check for nearly five thousand dollars and she gave a nervous laugh as she handed it over to the secretary. She felt like laughing, crying, and screaming all at once. *Maybe this is what insanity feels like*, Jess envisioned. The secretary handed her a receipt and called staff to inform them that Jess would be around to load up.

With everyone back in the truck and securely buckled, Jess began to carefully pull to the back of the facility where the neonatal unit was located.

"Mommy," Kat sang in her bright angel voice, "I can't wait to see the babies!"

"Me neither, Sweetie," Jess responded flatly. She wished she felt as elated as she should; however, regardless of donations that covered almost half of the bill, she felt increasingly uneasy ever since she wrote that check.

"Are you ok," Stephanie asked in concern, nervously eyeing the way Jess was rubbing her stomach.

Jess saw the worried expression on Stephanie's face and realized her friend was staring at her belly. "Yeah, I'm fine. It has all just been a little overwhelming for me," she said vaguely. Although there had been no talk of it at this point, Aiden watched his mother's face in the mirror and knew she was fighting with the thought of having to sell the twins. He desperately wished that there was something he could do to help her.

All worries were temporarily dashed out of the window when they rounded the corner and saw Dr. Linton along with several members of the New Bolton staff standing with Mona and their little miracles. "I forgot how tiny they are!" Stephanie whispered in awe.

"Ohhhhh!!!!! They are sooooooo cuuuuute!" Kat squealed in three-year-old glee. "Can I hug them? Please!" Kat pleaded.

"As soon as we get home, you may, Honey. Right now, we need to get them loaded up."
Jess eased the truck into park and she and Stephanie opened the doors to the truck.

"We want to get out, too," Aiden and Kat demanded.

"No!" Both women emphatically squashed any further attempts of escape simultaneously.

The kids sulked in the back while Jess and Stephanie spoke briefly with everyone. Dr. Linton was present with two bags, each labeled with a boy's name. She explained about the antibiotics each twin would need and other pertinent discharge information. Having spent most of the past ten days inside, the colts blinked in the bright sunlight and sniffed the warm air. Mona pawed anxiously and the children squealed in back of the truck with equal impatience.

Jessica tossed the bags of medications and discharge instructions on the worn seat of the truck and then turned back to load her precious cargo. Mona followed her onto the trailer without
hesitation and the staff members had the twins loaded before the mare could fret.

*   *   *

The joy of the homecoming was darkened by the observation of the colts' deformed legs once they were off the trailer. When Jessica last saw them, they were very weak in their rear pasterns, weak to the point that their little ankles actually touched the ground and the unknowing eye would think them crippled.

Their knees had also been hyper extended at birth, bending a few degrees behind a solid, straight line. The vision they all took in when the fragile foals stumbled off the trailer; however, shocked everyone present.

"Mommy!" Aiden nearly screamed in panic. "Their legs! What is wrong with their legs?"

Weak joints aside, the boys had exhibited wonderful, straight conformation in their legs in the first two days. Now, however, their legs were wickedly windswept. Viewed from the front, the long forearms and cannons, typically straight bones, actually *curved* out to the right and back in. Jess stifled a bit of a gag and held her left hand over her mouth as they began walking; their motion looked like some distorted paddling shuffle. Legs that should have rotated forward at the shoulder instead swung drunkenly to the right.

"Oh my gosh," Stephanie whispered under her breath.

They watched silently as the little babies scooted around the pasture. Unaware of the deformity that had developed in their legs, the twins happily bounced alongside their mother and sniffed at the tall grass in the pasture. They delighted in all of the new smells, sounds and sights.

"They will be fine." Jess reassured herself by caressing her growing belly. "They will straighten back out; I know they will."

"Yes, they will strengthen again," Stephanie echoed.

Jennifer Wilson

Chapter Twenty-One

June 29th - July 5th

Although summer was coming in full bloom, Mother Nature bestowed upon the fragile colts great mercy with moderate temperatures and sunshine filtered by gentle clouds. The twins enjoyed their brief exercises outside immensely. The Woman gradually increased their time outside and over the course of the week, they played harder and ran faster. Together, the little twins bounded across the pasture, finding joy in racing each other and kicking at shadows. The little fair-haired one never strayed too far from his dam, however. Through their play, their joints and tendons developed and strengthened. With each passing glorious day, their twisted legs because more correct and the colts grew more exquisite as they filled out. True to their Arabian heritage, they boasted strong hips and deep barrels; they were becoming beautiful examples of their breed's type. The chestnut mare proudly paraded around her fantastic creations, but she longed to be reunited with her fellow broodmares. The Woman gently assured her that soon, they would all be on turnout together.

Two times a day, The Woman and The Man would come in the large stall and force a bitter liquid down the throats of the colts. The People tried to be as gentle as possible. The larger, darker colt took the treatment in stride as he thoroughly enjoyed the human contact and was very social; the smaller, fairer colt, however, dreaded the treatment and took great offense. He began to shy from The People and his attempts to seek safety behind his mother's side became more frequent and increasingly panicked.

Jennifer Wilson

Jennifer Wilson

Chapter Twenty-Two

July 6th- June 10th

Jess smiled with satisfaction at the strength Majus and Majician had developed over the previous week. They were now up to a few hours' turn out each day. Although Mona was accustomed to full day turnout, she handled the limited time outside beautifully. Jessica was anxiously awaiting results from blood work Dr. Hanebutt ran earlier that morning. Today, Jess used the last of the antibiotics for the boys and the results of this test would determine if they would require another round of the medication or if they were in the clear. If they were in the clear, they would be able to have full day turnout. Playing all day would ensure that they would quickly grow strong enough to join the Half Arab babies. Jessica noticed how the different foals would look at each other in curiosity across the fences. She longed to see them all together and she knew that Mona wanted to be reunited with her mare companions.

Jessica also collected mane hairs from each colt this morning to mail in for DNA examination. The test would determine if they were identical or not. All who had seen them, including their vets, were certain they were identical. Although many of the Facebook fans noted that while their markings were very close, they were not exact. Some keen-eyed followers also saw their slight structural differences. Jessica found herself explaining a number of times how the genetic markers that determine the presence of a marking, a sock or a blaze, only determine just that- the existence of the marking. Even with clones, the exact expression of the markings are never exactly the same. There were only a handful of cases of identical twins in horses known in the world. She wasn't sure what she would do if they turned out identical. For the time being, she would just be happy with the fact that they were alive, healthy, and growing stronger every day.

After a good romp with his brother, Majus turned his attentions to the grass beneath his feet. His tiny, soft lips nibbled curiously at the thin blade. He had seen his mother and all of the other horses chewing on the grass for a week now, he was curious. Soon, Majician wandered over to see what his brother was so interested in. Within moments, both boys were mouthing the fine blades of grass with great intent, sharply nodding their little heads up and down in affirmation of the grass's sweet flavor.

A warm smile spread across Jess's face as she gazed upon this perfect scene of innocence and discovery. She had noted the previous night the twins were attempting to nibble at their dam's hay at the evening feeding. It was time for her to get some milk replacer pellets for the boys so that they could receive additional nourishment and take some of the strain off of Mona. She looked to be in amazing weight still, and the twins were filing out immensely, but Jessica was not sure just how long Mona would be able to produce for two growing boys.

*   *   *

"Jess," Matt said with concern later that night, "We can't keep them all. You know the plan was to sell Mona and the *foal* this year so you could focus on your Half Arabian program."

She sighed and looked at him, her eyes full of indecision and her voice pleading for patience. "I know. I know." She took a deep breath. "I have put some feelers out on a few Facebook sales pages and have had some inquiries. The problem is, I feel they *need* to stay together, but it is hard to find someone looking for a weanling colt, let alone two." She frowned. "I have about a dozen people that would snatch them up for $2,000 tomorrow. But I am tired of practically giving the horses away. Majus alone is worth ten times that. I have tried some three-in-one packages, but, again, can't seem to get more than $5,000 for the twins and Mona. I just can't do that. We have too much invested in them. And they are just so darned cool."

Matt could clearly see the pain in her face, and he didn't want to suggest that maybe she should concentrate on marketing the Half Arabian foals instead. She had developed a reputation as a top notch Half Arabian breeder and they would probably find quality show homes for those two far easier, and at a much greater profit. But he knew how much she wanted to finally show her magnificent Half Arabians herself. Not wanting to further stress his pregnant wife, he decided to let the matter drop for the time being.

*   *   *

The following morning, in the mid-afternoon, Dr. Hanebutt called to report that the blood work on the twins was almost normal. They were cleared from antibiotics. He was impressed with the strength their legs had developed and he also cleared them to have full day turnout. The boys could be introduced to the rest of the herd once Jess felt they were strong enough to keep up with the much larger and boisterous Half Arabian foals. So, they would survive. Tears of great relief ran down Jess's cheeks and her breath caught sharply in her chest as she stifled a little sob.

*   *   *

For the next several days, Jessica carefully watched the colts during their play outside. She saw that their previously bent spindly legs and weak joints continued to strengthen and straighten. By the end of the week, their legs almost appeared normal. Foals on both sides of the fence showed great interest in their neighbors. The big bay foals on the back side of the fence and the tiny chestnut twins on the front side of the fence raced each other from end to end. They would run until the sides of all four foals heaved as they greedily gulped the air into their strengthening lungs and their muscles quivered from exertion. The little racers would all return to their respective dams, have a quick snack and sink into the soft pasture for a refreshing nap. When they awoke, they would nibble contentedly at some grass until one would hear the crank of a lawn mower or the distant shot of a gun and they would be off, racing again with little tails held proudly over their backs like tiny banners. Jess was certain the little guys were ready to join the rest of the herd.

Chapter Twenty-Three

July 11th

For many days now, the two pairs of foals had examined, measured up, and tested each other across the fence line. They were immensely curious about each other and were impressed with one another's abilities. The chestnut mare took good care of her colts, but she dearly missed her herd companions, the black mare and the old grey mare. She was the dominant mare on the farm and it concerned her to be separated from her herd. She had been patient for her little colts, but they were becoming stronger and her separation agitation was growing daily. The weather, while warm, remained far cooler than typical for mid-July. The chestnut mare began pacing the fence line as her patience wore. The Woman had observed as this behavior escalated over several days and she knew the time had come to introduce the twins to rest of the herd.

Chapter Twenty-Four

July 11th

Jess waited until Saturday to make the big introduction. She wanted Matt to be there in case there was a mishap. She had more than enough experience with horses to know that dreadful accidents could easily result from ridiculously excited mares who forget about the tiny foal who is frantically running at its mother's side. Jess held little doubt that the mares would be excited to be reunited. Too excited, probably.

Matt, Aiden, and Kat stood impatiently at the back gate, ready to watch the integration of the twins into their herd. Jess took a deep breath and began with Sweetie and Jesse. Jesse, at only three weeks of age, had become quite the independent young colt. He was the least likely to follow his mother through the gate and cause some sort of traffic jam, or worse, an escape as he lingered around deciding whether he would follow his dam through or not. After several minutes of poking around, Jesse finally meandered through the open gate into the pasture to join his waiting mother. Jess unsnapped the lead line from the grey mare, gave her a quick pat on the shoulder and returned to the barn for Penny and her filly. The big black mare was annoyed at how long

136

she had waited since her pasture mate went out and she impatiently shoved Jess's hand aside when she first attempted to slip the halter over her head.

"Now look here," the tiny woman growled at the enormous creature in front of her. "I know he took forever getting through and you are impatient, but you aren't going out until you get your halter on."

Penny nodded her head sharply a few times, then gently lowered it so that Jess could reach without having to stand on her tip toes. The big black mare practically led herself to the gate while her filly daintily bounced at her shoulder. At the gate, Jess fussed at the impatient mare again.

"Knock it off, Penny. You stand still or we will have a little lesson on patience!"

Penny swished her tail and sighed in exasperation. After about a minute of standing quietly, Jess opened the gate and led the excited mare through. Hearing the click of leadline snap as Jess freed it from her halter, the young mare exploded out to her much older sister where, together, their foals bonded off with each other. Jess was awestruck, as always, for a few brief moments at the magnificence of the Half Arabian foals.

Her heart beat accelerating and her palms beginning to sweat, she turned back to retrieve Mona and the twins. Contained in her stall, Mona was tossing her head and pawing at the door.

She looked up at Jess and her long mane was draped across both sides of her neck and sections were hanging on the curvy tips of her ears. Jess quietly adjusted her mane to the correct side and smoothed it down. Mona bumped Jess with her muzzle. With a deep breath, Jess slid the halter over Mona's ears, snapped the throat latch, and swung the stall door open.

Majus and Majician bounced excitedly alongside their dam as Jess led them to the gate that opened to the larger pasture. As she had hoped, Sweetie and Penny had led their foals to the far end to graze near the shade of the woods line. *Thank goodness, I have plenty of time before we are spotted,* Jess thought. She quietly slipped the chain that secured the gate from around the post and swung it open into the pasture. She led Mona through and turned to see if the boys had followed. Majician, as expected, was glued to his mother's far side. Majus, on the other hand, had his own agenda. He was still sniffing around the open gate, taking in the idea that he would be permitted to enter this new domain.

Jess glanced nervously over her shoulder and saw that they had been spotted. Both Penny and Sweetie, heads held high, were staring intently at the trio standing by the open gate. *Come on,* Jess thought as Majus still milled around the open gate.

Majus, excited by the new possibilities, but independent enough to make his own decisions, flipped his tail over his back and pranced back and forth in front of the gate. He was taking his time and relishing every second. Sweetie and Penny, eyes bright and nostrils flaring, had taken a few indecisive steps forward. Jess saw Majus lift his head, she saw his eyes widen, she saw his nostrils flare, and she saw his throat latch tighten. She saw him suck in his breath. *No you don't!* Jess pleaded in her head. He did.

Majus's baby whinny carried far past the ears of his mother. Sweetie and Penny tensed. Mona, as a mother will, responded with a whinny of her own. Like thoroughbreds at The Derby as the bell clangs, Sweetie and Penny bolted from the far end of the pasture towards Mona, the split twins and the open gate. Quickly, Jess trotted Mona away from the open gate. Majus, seeing his mother heading away from him decided to stop dallying and shot through the gate. Jess faced Mona away from the open gate, now some ten yards behind her, unsnapped the lead line and ran as fast as her loosening joints and pregnant belly would allow her. She heard the sound of thunder fast approaching as the three groups of mares and foals drew nearer each other. Jess made it to the gate, slammed it shut, flung the chain around the post, and turned to view the spectacle of the introduction.

She sucked in her breath as the seven horses snorted and blew. Their necks proudly arched and their tails were banners in the wind. The foal's tails curled right over their backs and they strutted like peacocks, each trying to out show the others. A few mareish squeals sounded as dominance and pecking order were quickly reestablished and then the small herd took off across the open back pasture. At the far end, Jess could see Aiden and Kat standing on the gate, grinning, and clapping their hands in delight. Even Matt, inwardly concerned about his wife's willingness to part with any of these foals, was grinning broadly. For the next several minutes, mares and foals delighted in their fiery dance. The air resounded with the echoes of pounding hooves and snorts and blows. The mares arched their necks like stallions and the foals waved their tails proudly in the air. Finally, the phenomenal display wound down and the seven ethereal creatures returned to the mortal world. They walked themselves out quietly, sucking in huge gulps of air into their expansive lungs. After a few minutes, their once banner-like tails lowered and resumed their primal purpose of quietly swishing flies and they dropped their heads to contentedly graze the sweet grass beneath their hooves. It was then that Jess realized that she had been so enchanted by the show that she failed to take her phone out of her pocket and video what was one of the most glorious displays of equine beauty that she had ever witnessed.

Majus and Majician - The BOGO Arabian colts
July 12, 2015 · 🌐

Yesterday, the boys were introduced to the rest of the broodmare herd, much to Mona's relief. All three mares can get silly from time to time, but they are great moms and Mona is a very reasonable lead mare. Her BFF is the black half Arab mare and they were very happy to be reunited. All foals get along tremendously well and all moms are tolerant of all babies. This video is of today ... Yesterday involved a large amount of tail flagging, snorting and extreme showing off, but my main concern was making sure they mixed harmoniously rather than snagging video. They are a happy crew!

169,311 people reached   **Boost Post**

37K Views

👍 Like   💬 Comment   ↗ Share   🖼 ▾

○ Jennifer Al-Beik, Katie Merrick and 1.4K others   Chronological ▾

Chapter Twenty-Five

July 12th - August 4th

Over the next several weeks, the little foals grew. The summer sun shone down intensely. The days got hotter and the bothersome horseflies, early summer pests, subsided. Jess grew, too. Her pregnant stomach swelled with the baby. The baby became increasingly active and Jess became increasingly uncomfortable. Despite the heat and the discomfort, Jess still made it out every morning to feed the horses and every few days, she made a video or snapped some pictures to share with the twins' loyal Facebook fans.

On July 20th, Jess received an email from the genetics laboratory. She felt a sharp rush of adrenaline as she opened the attached file. Although there was no letter of explanation attached, a quick glance at the genetic markers on the brothers told her they clearly were not identical. Jess was dumbfounded. It wasn't that she expected to have identical twins, that would make them the rarest horses on Earth. She was more amazed at how similar they were in their markings and more perplexed with how they were situated inside their mother's uterus. She texted the results to the two vets who worked the most with them, Dr. Dayton and Dr. Linton. They were not exactly expecting identical twins either, but

Majus and Majician - The BOGO Arabian colts
July 18, 2015 ·

Happy 1 month birthday Bo and Luke!!! Today is also the party for my 8 year old son, so I'm going crazy getting ready for that. Here's a quickie video, unedited so no cute music and pardon my clicking and smooching 😊 They are getting so much stronger and are looking more and more like "normal" foals. It's crazy to see them developing and losing that tiny preemie look. Bo (Majician) is starting to shed his foal coat, so will start looking a little mangy soon. Can't wait to see them all shed out and slick!

134,256 people reached   **Boost Post**

31K Views

👍 Like   💬 Comment   ➤ Share

⭕ Kari Goings, Jennifer Al-Beik and 984 others   Chronological ▾

1,068 shares

they were just as bewildered with the specifics of the colts' gestation and uncanny resemblance to each other. No one was able to answer how they developed inside the same placenta if they were fraternal twins.

In early August, Matt finally gave up his hope that his wife would find a suitable home for some of the horses in a timely manner.

"Jess," he said one night, "I am really worried about you selling the foals. Have you even listed them anywhere?"

"I've put out some feelers," Jess replied sullenly. "The twins just *have* to stay together if we sell them. I don't know how I will ever find a home that will take *two* colts. They can't go to just any home, either. And the Half Arabs would have to go to a serious show home. Our program can't fizzle out once Maghnus retires. I'm trying."

"I know you haven't been serious because you haven't clipped any of them out. I don't even know how you plan to clip out foals this big that aren't halter broke. Especially in your condition. You can barely clean stalls anymore. Baby, you aren't as young as you were with Aiden."

Matt's face doubled and then swam in her vision. She tried to swallow the hard lump that had swelled in her throat. He had called her out on her procrastination and laid on the table her situation which had previously gone understood but unspoken. In a tight, strained voice she tried to explain to him that she didn't want to practically give the horses away. The look on his face told her that he had heard that story too many times before and she dropped her eyes.

"I'll post an ad on Mona tomorrow. There are so many mare buyers, it shouldn't take long."

Although the plan had originally been to get one more great filly out of Mona and then sell her and the foal for good prices to support the Half Arabian program, she had secretly hoped that the "filly" would sell for enough to allow her to just lease Mona for a year or two while they were building the new farm up. She had spent the past several weeks avoiding both her husband and the nagging little accountant in the back of her head.

Even though a quiet ultimatum had been called Jess drug her feet for a couple more weeks before listing the copper-colored treasure. She knew in her heart that she would never be able to replace the mare once the farm was complete and their lives were more firmly on the ground. She also knew that she had to sell at least two foals. She couldn't bear to part with any of them, but she recognized the fact that the Half Arabians would be easier sales than the twins; she was firm that the boys would not be sold to separate homes. She ordered some sedative from Dr. Dayton, and with Matt's help, she managed to clip the necks and faces of the twins and the lovely filly, Cali.

Jennifer Wilson

Chapter Twenty-Six

August 5th - August 25th

Finally, the day came that Jess knew she would no longer be able to put off listing Mona for sale. There had still been no serious interest in any of the foals for prices reflective of their quality. She found a few good photographs of her and a great video with the twins that truly showcased the mare's athleticism and fiery charm. She posted these on Facebook and a few online equine sales sites with the mare's registered name, PA A-Magic Moment.

Within a few days, the inquiries were coming in on the gorgeous mare who had effortlessly carried, delivered, and nourished twins. Jessica was able to sift through most of the tire-kickers, those "professional" shoppers who seemed like they were always shopping and never buying. She had several potential buyers who wanted to offer half the price she was asking but Jess was not yet ready to negotiate. She held her ground on the price. Partially because the mare was worth well more than her list price. Partially because she needed every penny to set up her new farm and hold onto the hope of keeping either the twins or the half Arabian foals. Mostly, though, it was because her heart wasn't ready to let go of the mare she knew was a once in a lifetime.

On August 24th, as life often happens, it stopped raining and began pouring. Jessica received a phone call from someone local who wanted to come see the mare that evening. When her phone rang a few hours later, someone else from a few hours away wanted to come see her that weekend. Jess explained that a local woman was coming that evening to see her, she would call her back if it didn't work out. An hour before the scheduled appointment, Jess received a Facebook message from a third woman who wanted to buy her sight-unseen. Jessica explained to Veronica that local people were scheduled to see the mare, but she would be in contact as soon as they left.

The two women messaged back and forth, and by the time the potential buyers were due to arrive, Jessica prayed they wouldn't show because this woman from Facebook was the perfect home for her priceless mare.

Jess's heart fell when she saw the truck pull into the drive. She messaged Veronica that the people had arrived and that she would let her know the outcome ASAP. Veronica, feeling drawn by fate, responded that if the people were interested and agreed to the sale price that she would offer more than the advertised price. Jess's heart skipped a couple of beats as she realized that no matter how the sale presentation turned out, Mona would be sold by the time she returned to the house.

Jennifer Wilson

Jess took one look at the prospective buyers, and in her heart knew they were not the right people for Mona. They were friendly, kind, and exuded an overall gentle personality. They were fans of natural horsemanship. They had left the world of Quarter Horses behind and purchased a couple of Arabians. Now, they were looking to improve their breeding program. On the surface, nothing existed to raise a red flag; Jess simply knew in her heart they weren't right.

After looking the mare over and admiring the twins for what seemed like a week, the couple said she was nice and they would think it over. They said they would be in touch over the weekend. Jess never heard from them again. She watched them pull out of the drive, whipped her phone out of her pocket, and informed Veronica that a sale was not made to them. Within five minutes, the full asking price of the mare was sitting in her Paypal account. She wrote the sales contract with various emotions swirling in her heart and the women discussed the time of weaning, their schedules, and worked out a future date in the fall where Veronica would pick Mona up and take her to her new home.

All of Jessica's misgivings about letting Mona go were dashed away when she received a message from Lori the following day.

"Did I read correctly that her barn nick name is Mona?"

153

Jennifer Wilson

"Yes! She's Mona! Or any pet variation of that, lol. Mone-baloney, Momee, etc...lol"

Jess was curious about the significance of the barn name for only a few moments. Veronica went on to explain that earlier that year she lost the nicest mare she had ever had. Her barn name had been Mona.

"When I read her nickname in the Twins article I cried and got goose bumps."

For as broken as Jess's heart was, it seemed the Lord had had a plan all along.

Chapter Twenty-Seven

August 26th-September 15th

Jessica was due on September 6th. She prayed this daughter would not be as stubborn as Kat, who not only was ten days overdue, but also decided to arrive on her own ten hours before the scheduled induction. It just happened to be Superbowl Sunday. Jess was not getting any younger, and this baby promised to be large. Although she carried on her daily duties, her discomfort had become extreme. To add salt to the wound, school had also begun the previous week. Jessica's maternity leave was scheduled for September 6th or whenever the baby arrived; whichever came first. Her students and co-workers were incredibly supportive as she waddled down the halls and took many breaks. She did her best, but her energy was fading. She barely had energy to even look at the horses and Matt took over much of the daily care. Although Jess had been having contractions for weeks, the baby's due date came and went. Her maternity leave began and she waited. And waited. The doctors scheduled an induction for September fourteenth.

Jess felt she would never make it that long; however, on the fourteenth of September, nothing felt different and by that evening

Jennifer Wilson

Aiden and Kat were packed off to their grandfather, Janine was headed to the hospital and Jess found Matt and herself signing them in for the induction. Paperwork done, she prepared for the triage nurse to perform the pre-exam.

"Oh, honey! You are in labor! There's no induction here! Weren't you having contractions?"

"No," Jess replied, tears pricking at her eyes. She felt her veins turn to ice and began trembling. "Nothing felt any worse than what I have had for the past five weeks." Her time had come, and, as twice before, she was terrified.

Twelve hours later, she cradled a beautiful, almost nine pound bundle of baby girl in her arms.

Chapter Twenty-Eight

September

The days grew shorter and the hot hazy temperatures melted to glorious fall crispness. The mares relished the cooler weather and the pesky summer mosquitoes faded away.

Together, the four foals frolicked and grew and grew. They all were eating their own hay and grain in addition to nursing from their dams. Their sleek, glistening summer coats grew thicker as the nights grew longer. The half Arabian foals were huge for their ages, and although they dwarfed the much smaller twins, Majus and Majician had also grown remarkably. Every so often, an observer could get a glimpse of the fine stallion Majus was destined to become and the sleek show gelding waiting to develop in Majician. In the crisp evenings, the firefly light shows gave way to the chorus of the crickets. The horses did not see The Woman much at all anymore, but The Man was taking good care of them. The four, growing each day, remained friendly, but untrained and essentially wild. They were blissful in their ignorance that very soon, they would be weaned from their mothers and their carefree lives would be forever changed.

Chapter Twenty-Nine

September-October

Jessica spent a week healing from the delivery of sweet Sarah. She spent the next few weeks just enjoying being a mother. She relished in snuggling and cuddling what was sure to be her last baby. She kissed and cooed. The house work waited. The horses waited. Jess had little time to really think about how four untrained foals would be halter broken. She had little time to think about how they would successfully wean the foals from their dams with only three stalls and nine horses. For now, there was only Sarah.

"Jess, you know it's about time to wean these babies. Lori wants to pick Mona up right after Nationals in the first week of November."

"I know, honey," Jess responded. She was sitting in the rocking chair and gazing down at the sleeping baby wrapped in a soft, pink blanket. "Isn't she beautiful?"

"Jess, what are your plans?" Matt implored. He usually didn't ask horse related questions, but he needed to know. Once Mona left, they would still have eight horses. Far too many than they could handle over the winter with their current setup. Not to mention the fact that the sale of Mona combined with the GoFundMe drive was only enough to bring them back to ground zero. He knew what the answer would be. He didn't like it, but he knew it was the only way.

"I'm going to have to take them to the Wolfes. Resi can halter break and they can handle the weaning better than we can."

Well, there goes being back to ground zero, Matt thought. They had weaned Cali, the Half Arabian filly, that weekend and had sent her mother to Tennessee to complete her under saddle training with David Conner. This would be a minimum of a six month financial obligation. He sighed and wondered how long the twins would be boarded at the trainers; he knew they didn't have enough stalls for all of the foals, and he knew Jess was still torn over which foals to sell. He also knew she was going to hold out for a good price on any of them for several more months.

Jess's internal accountant scowled and jotted down a note. She stuck it to the wall of Jess's brain. *YOU need to do something about this. YOU need to make something BIG happen.*

Jess smiled down at the content pink bundle breathing deeply in her lap, and for the time being, continued to ignore reality and her sense of fiscal responsibility.

* * *

In mid-October, Jess brought Mona home from the Wolfes and Majus and Majician were weaned from their mother. Two days later, Veronica picked up the beautiful chestnut mare to bring her home to Ohio. Aiden and Kat had said their goodbyes the evening before but, against Jess's wishes, they insisted on seeing her onto the trailer. Jess fought back the tears with all she had; she needed to be strong for her children who were racked with deep sobs of grief. They were accustomed to selling the foals; they were not accustomed to selling their beloved mares. Aiden's face was pale and swollen from the intensity of his crying and great red blotches spread across his pasty cheeks. Jessica allowed them one more kiss through the window of the trailer, gave Veronica a hug, and watched her copper treasure pull out to a new home and a new life.

Within a week, Majestik was also weaned and went to live with Resi for a while so he could be separated from his dam and halter broken.

Chapter Thirty

November-February

Over what remained of that year, Jessica was completely overwhelmed with her return to work from maternity. She had a hundred high school students with whom to familiarize herself in a very short time. As a Special Education teacher, she also had thirteen students to whom she needed to introduce herself as case manager. She found herself in the position to write three new IEPs in the first three weeks of her return and several more breathing down her back following those. The half Arabian foals were brought back home and shared the large stall in inclement weather. Before she could blink, Christmas had come and gone and it was 2016. Her trainer in Tennessee, David Conner, moved back to Delaware and, soon, the half Arabian foals joined the black mare in training there so they could be clipped and marketed. The twins came home from the Wolfes' farm in early January, but they were still not weaned from each other. They shared a stall and, while sweet, they were not easy for Jessica to manage in the current farm set-up.

Jess did the best she could, but she knew it wasn't enough. Even with a Masters Degree, a teacher's salary only goes so far,

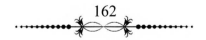

and she had promised herself that Matt had supported her long enough. The horse bills were astronomical and she knew she was in far over her head. She was putting the growth of her farm in jeopardy. Something had to give.

In late January, she posted on the twin's Facebook page about selling the half-Arabian foals in order to keep the twins together. This post spun into a supportive discussion that built a second revolution of support for the colts. Ideas were churned out; everything from selling calendars to contacting TV shows to raffles. PayPal information was posted and within days, enough donations were received to cover two months of training for each colt. These generosities gave Jess a little breathing room, but, while inspirational, they were merely short term fixes. *There just has to be something I can do. There has to be!*

And then someone posted on their page, *You know, this story could be a movie.*

Jess stared blankly at the old laptop screen and blinked a few times as she moved inwards to herself. She wandered through the cluttered hallways of her mind's idea room. She moved further and further back until she reached the desk of her little internal accountant. She sighed at the stacks and stacks of papers littering the desk and the massive files and folders. Jess's eye caught a bright yellow square plastered to the wall and was drawn to it. The words scrawled on the note read, *"YOU need to do something about this. YOU need to make something BIG happen."* But what? What could she do? Jess fingertips rubbed her forehead, as if they were attempting to stimulate some mental action. *You know, this story could be a movie.* A furtive smile played along the corners of her mouth and she chewed gently on her lower lip. Yes, she could do something. She could do something big. Something that would make all of her dreams a reality *and* share to the world the beauty of hope and the endless possibilities of living one's dreams.

And so, on the first snow day of the year, with Baby Sarah sleeping soundly and Aiden and Kat contentedly watching cartoons downstairs, Jess, settled into the favorite beige rocking chair of her mother-in-law, got to work. The snow silently drifted down outside the magnificent plate glass window that ran the length of the living room. She tucked her legs under her, shifted her old computer on her lap, and with a nervous smile and a heart full of hope, she began to type the story of Majus and Majician, starting with her 36th birthday when she discovered that she would be expecting three foals in the summer of 2015.

Epilogue

Presently

At the time of the first printing, the boys are thriving at David Conner's farm. I visit them weekly. They are growing and growing. Majus looks like he will make a fine stallion. I am currently considering gelding Majician. For one, I don't need two stallions that are full brothers. Also, I can't show two stallions at once. Finally, by gelding Majician, the boys will still be able to enjoy turn out time together. That could be a complicated situation with two stallions.

We have sold the beautiful filly, Cali. She will remain in training with David Conner for many years to come, so I get to see her frequently as well. We have Sweetie's amazing colt in training, too, and he is currently on the market. I have been avoiding my poor husband's quiet inquiries regarding any sales leads on him. I hold out hope that this book goes viral immediately upon its release and I will not have to sell him after all. I figure, at the time of writing this, I can get away with about three more weeks before I have to bring him home. Sweetie is due in mid-June. As she is twenty now, I have to keep in my mind that this could very well be her last foal. I remain completely determined to keep the twins and ride out this adventure with which I have been blessed.

It amazes me how many lives these twins have touched. I have received countless messages about the joy and inspiration they have given people. I hope this story helps more people have the courage to chase their dreams. To be cliché, life is simply too short not to.

Recent Photographs

Jennifer Wilson

Jennifer Wilson

Jennifer Wilson

Jennifer Wilson

Jennifer Wilson

The Fans

Majus and Majician - The BOGO Arabian colts

👍 Like Page

February 24 · 🌐

Ok... sooooo.... if you have ever commented on a post and would or would not mind your comment to maybe be in print, please let me know. I am making a cool feature in the book. I want to pre-narrow-down a list each of folks who would be ok forever being printed in heir book and those who would prefer to be blacked out. This book will be over the top ☹

4,324 people reached | **Boost Post**

👍 Like   💬 Comment   ➤ Share   ▾

⭕⭕👤 Angela Norton, Hellen J Ferguson and 355 others   Chronological ˙

View previous comments   49 of 260

 Shelly Wood I Love These Boys!!! So Beautiful & Care Free!!! U Have Done A Wonderful Job Raising These Two Boogers!!! Your More Than Welcome To Use Any Of My Comments, And Your Book Will Be One Of A Kind Good For U!!!
Like · Reply · Message · February 25 at 10:33am

Emily Bee Use mine if you like!
Like · Reply · Message · February 25 at 10:53am

Kamie Grant Burton I'm good with it
Like · Reply · Message · February 25 at 11:40am · Edited

Lauren Wood I'm fine with it! 🙂
Like · Reply · Message · February 25 at 12:07pm

Gillian Howell I am perfectly fine with that, to be remotely associated with these miracles is a once in a lifetime thing 🙂
Like · Reply · Message · February 25 at 12:25pm

Anne Winters I loved watching the twins grow
Like · Reply · Message · February 25 at 12:30pm

Anne Winters I am okay with it
Like · Reply · Message · February 25 at 12:30pm

Lorel Berg Reasonably certain I have made several comments. Love these two. Us any or all of whatever I may have written

Like · Reply · Message · February 25 at 1:50pm

 Stephanie Primm I'm ok with it! Can't wait to see sneak peaks of the book 😀
Like · Reply · Message · February 25 at 2:01pm

 Cyndy-Lou S. Hancock It would be good with me but can you let the individuals know so they can look forward to seeing it in print ... 😊 👢 🎵
Like · Reply · Message · February 25 at 2:14pm

 Liz Kulis I don't mind at all!! I love these boys 🖤 🖤 🖤
Like · Reply · Message · February 25 at 2:21pm

 Lorraine Neil i dont mind
Like · Reply · Message · February 25 at 2:56pm

 Brenda Rogers Love seeing them grow!!!
Like · Reply · Message · February 25 at 3:28pm

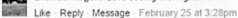

 Patricia Swaim Fine with me I love those guys
Like · Reply · Message · February 25 at 3:31pm

 Savannah Carling I'm ok too.
Like · Reply · Message · February 25 at 3:44pm

 Angela Dillon That's okay with me, I love horses. even though I have never owned one myself, but worked for a man who had some, when I was in high school, which is where my love of horses started.
Like · Reply · Message · February 25 at 3:46pm

 Sonya Dittemore I am good with it
Like · Reply · Message · February 25 at 6:43pm

 Helaina Kanzer Love these babies. I'm ok with the using of any of my comments
Like · Reply · Message · February 25 at 6:58pm

 Marty Nicol They are beautiful babies...I'm in. 😀
Like · Reply · Message · February 25 at 7:42pm

 Lanette Martin I'm Ok with it, anything for the boys!
Like · Reply · Message · February 25 at 7:58pm

Lj Ide I'm okay with that
Like · Reply · Message · February 25 at 8:23pm

Jennifer Wilson

 Judy Keefe I would love to be in their book!!
Like · Reply · Message · February 25 at 9:38pm

 Linda Leslie I can't recall if I ever commented but I have followed you from the beginning. What a journey.
Like · Reply · Message · February 25 at 9:50pm

 Michelle Guy I'm fine with u using mine !!!
Like · Reply · Message · February 25 at 9:57pm

 Patty Ann Younker I'm okay with it.
Like · Reply · Message · February 25 at 10:28pm

 Charisse Lewis I don't mind a bit
Like · Reply · Message · February 25 at 10:46pm

 Renee Molnes I'm okay with it.
Like · Reply · Message · February 25 at 11:14pm

 Meribeth Dermond I love them!! You can use any comments photos etc.
Like · Reply · Message · February 25 at 11:39pm

 Siri Carlson Don't know what I have commented but please do.
Unlike · Reply · Message · 👍 1 · February 25 at 11:41pm

 Lindsey Reid I'm ok
Like · Reply · Message · February 26 at 12:02am

 Debbie Lucero Hernandez iwould love i have followed u since the boys were born i lve them
Like · Reply · Message · February 26 at 12:41am

 Christina Marie Crowell I would love to be in their book
Like · Reply · Message · February 26 at 12:53am

 Elizabeth Bonbright Feel free. Love these boys!
Like · Reply · Message · February 26 at 1:31am

 Lisa Siegwald-Baird Ditto !
Like · Reply · Message · February 26 at 4:21am

 Linda Dudgeon Ok here...have enjoyed watching these guys grow up and thrive....hope they are never seperated!
Unlike · Reply · Message · 👍 1 · February 26 at 9:10am

 Judy Klingenhofer I would never post something on Facebook that I don't want someone to see 😊 so it's good.
Unlike · Reply · Message · 👍 1 · February 26 at 11:08am

 Jennifer McGuire I'm good with it!
Like · Reply · Message · February 26 at 11:27am

Ellen Nobles Ilove your site and would never post anything I did not want printed. I had an Arabian when I was younger and love to see yours and read about them. Thank you,
Unlike · Reply · Message · 👍 1 · February 27 at 11:16am

 Whitney Smith I'm good with it 🙂
Like · Reply · Message · February 27 at 6:18pm

 Kate Walters If I ever said anything worthy of being remembered, I'm fine with it. That said, I can't imagine actually being profoundly interesting when it comes to postings. 🙂
Like · Reply · Message · February 27 at 6:33pm

 Cheyenne Nicole Hanson I dont know if I ever commented but I dont mind if I have!
Like · Reply · Message · February 27 at 7:17pm

 Rachel Clemmer I'm good with it!
Like · Reply · Message · February 27 at 7:30pm

 Jonell Kelm This horse lover totally doesn't mind. The boys are so special. Thank you for sharing them with us!
Like · Reply · Message · February 28 at 5:56pm

 Cindy LeBlanc I don't mind if you use my post as I think your twin colts are awesome both in personality and of course their matched colours! I myself have loved and studied Arabian horses for many years now and they will always be a passion of mine. I have always loved your videos on the twin colts and feel that you are doing everything possible to support their well being. Looking forward to their progress!
Like · Reply · Message · February 28 at 6:07pm

 Heather Curry Yes, that would be fine.
Like · Reply · Message · February 29 at 12:12am

 Valerie L Cooper If there was anything you'd like to include that I commented on, I am ok with that. 🙂 I LOVE those two colts! 💚
Like · Reply · Message · February 29 at 1:03am

 Terry Naylor Black I don't mind! They have been my lifeline since they were born, watching their clumsiness when they were so young and today seeing how they have grown so much and getting so elegant with every step they take, THANK YOU SO MUCH FOR SHARING!! God Bless you for the joy you have given so many of us!!
Like · Reply · Message · March 27 at 10:17pm

 Donna Icelandic I have made comments,okay with anything you print!!!
Like · Reply · Message · 24 mins

 Write a comment...

Mark Corbin

08/06/2015 3:17PM

Thank You Thank You Thank You
for the daily updates on the Twins!
That's my Smile for the Day! I do
Look Forward to them!

08/09/2015 11:18AM

You are starting to get the picture of what your videos and words mean to us all. You've done an amazing job with them!

I'm going to see one day that I can make that dream come true!

THANK you so much for replying to my message! I was not expecting you to do that! You are a very busy person I am SURE!!! I just want you to know what a gift you have given all of us with your videos.. They will stay in my heart forever. No reply nessesary 😊

Jennifer Wilson

Sa Ransone

As I shoveled snow it got me thinking about the marguerite Henry books. Need to find an author to write their story in a series so that little girls and big can look for the next one!!

JAN 24TH, 5:21PM

Ohhh.... I'm actually an English teacher and a pretty darned decent writer. Hmmm.... It wouldn't be able to be 100% accurate because it would need a main conflict with heroes (kids) to solve, but it sure could be based on them!!!

Get a few heads together, I'm sure there is a seried

series

And it's fiction so

make the reader wait for another tsle

Wishing you the best of luck....karma let them live for a reason......hang in there Jennifer......our horses always tug at our heart strings.....you boys have captured the hearts of the world.....ps your other foals (including the 2 legged ones) are Gorgeous!!! I have a stunning home bred 4yr Arabian warmblood beginning under saddle .....he's the love of my life and more than I thought according to outsiders in the know who have seen him.....know just how you feel about your fur babies!

Maggie Trees Souders

08/24/2015 9:39AM

I wanted to let you know that your videos are pretty much the highlight of my 19 month old sons life! Every single night we watch them over and over and over (and over) again. I keep meaning to video him watching your videos. He is absolutely fixated on them. Thank you so much for all the video diaries of those precious twins!
On a side note, I am great friends with Maddy Winer, and we are HUGE Magnus fans! And Rosie (I think that's what you called her???) The grey yearling fully Maddy purchased from you, is at my mothers farm. She sure is a pretty filly!!
Good luck with the pregnancy, and I look forward to all the upcoming videos!

Jennifer Wilson

Majus and Majician

follow them on Facebook

www.facebook.com/bogocolts

follow future book releases

www.facebook.com/bogocoltsbook

see all of their videos,

from the beginning on Youtube

The BOGO Colts

order their annual calendar

http://www.lulu.com/spotlight/majusmajician

Jennifer Wilson

About the Author

Jennifer Wilson is a special education high school teacher. She was always that horse-crazy girl for as long as she can remember and has been involved in Arabian horses for almost thirty years. She and her husband, Mark, founded Zenith Farms in 2004 with the purchase of the Half Arabian mare, The Sweet Rose. In 2006, they welcomed their first foal, a filly out of Sweetie. As of 2015, The Sweet Rose has produced seven outstanding foals for the farm, including one of the most successful Half Arabian halter geldings in history, Maghnus Z. With only four foals actively showing, the youngest maturing before they hit the ring, her progeny have won 18 National Champions or Reserve Championships, an additional eight National Top 10s and over 30 Regional Champion or Reserve Championships.

Jennifer lives in Milford, Delaware with her husband and three children, Austin, Kate, and Savannah. This book is Jennifer's first novel. She hopes in the future to create a fictional series for young teens based on the adventures of the twins, Majus and Majician.

Jennifer Wilson